F A I R Y

T A L E

FAIRY TALE

CYN BALOG

Delacorte Press

Copyright © 2009 by Cyn Balog
All rights reserved. Published in the United States by Delacorte Press,
an imprint of Random House Children's Books, a division of
Random House, Inc., New York.

Delacorte Press is a registered trademark and the colophon is a
trademark of Random House, Inc.

Visit us on the Web! www.randomhouse.com/teens

Educators and librarians, for a variety of teaching tools,
visit us at www.randomhouse.com/teachers

Library of Congress Cataloging-in-Publication Data
Balog, Cyn.
   Fairy tale / Cyn Balog. — 1st ed.
      p. cm.
   Summary: Morgan Sparks and her boyfriend Cam have been best
friends since they were children, but just before their shared sixteenth
birthday Cam confesses that he is a fairy who was switched at birth with
a human child, and now the fairies want to switch them back.
   ISBN 978-0-385-73706-7 (trade) — ISBN 978-0-385-90644-9 (lib.
bdg.) — ISBN 978-0-375-89102-1 (e-book)
   [1. Fairies—Fiction. 2. Changelings—Fiction. 3. High schools—Fiction.
4. Schools—Fiction.] I. Title.
   PZ7.B2138Fai 2009
   [Fic]—dc22
                        2008035665

The text of this book is set in 11-point Baskerville Book.

Printed in the United States of America

10 9 8 7 6 5 4 3

First Edition

For Sara

ACKNOWLEDGMENTS

I don't have fairy powers, but I know this book wouldn't be possible without the help of some amazing people I'm pretty sure *do* have them.

Thank you to all the writers I've met online, especially the Why Eh Writers and the 2009 Debs. I'm eternally grateful to my writing BFF, Mandy Hubbard, and to Brooke Taylor for keeping me sane day after day. Thanks to Nadia Cornier for believing in *Fairy Tale* when it was just a glimmer. To my editor, Stephanie Lane, copy editor Kate Oschner, cover designer Marci Senders, and everyone at Delacorte Press for taking a chance on *Fairy Tale* and making it shine brighter than I ever imagined it could. To Mom and Dad for buying me that desk and word processor and for never forcing me to "go out and get some fresh air" when I wanted to write. To Jen, the inspiration for my early writing pursuits . . . where would *My sister Jen is talented* be without you? To my husband, Brian, for having unwavering faith in me, and to Sara for filling every one of my days with smiles. Thanks for the wings.

1

PEOPLE CALL ME spooky.

Maybe because by eleven o'clock on that day, I'd already told Ariana Miles she'd starve to death in Hollywood, Erica Fuentes she'd bomb history, and Wendell Marks that he would never, ever be a part of the A-list, no matter how hard he tried.

Now, sitting in the bleachers after school, half watching a meaningless Hawks football exhibition game and waiting for some nameless freshman to bring me my French fries (psychics cannot work on an empty stomach), I've just about reduced my fourth client of the day to tears (well, Wendell didn't cry; he just pretended to yawn, covered his mouth, and let out a pathetic snurgle). But hey, sometimes the future is scary.

Sierra Martin won't look at me. Instead, she's taken an

unnatural interest in the Heath bar wrapper wedged between the metal planks her sequin-studded flip-flops are resting on. A tear slips past her fake-tanned knees and lands perfectly on her porno-red big-toe nail.

"Sorry," I say, offering her a pat on the back and a couple of orange Tic Tacs for consolation. "Really."

Sometimes this gift does suck. Some days, I have the pleasure of doling out good news—BMWs as graduation presents, aced finals, that sort of thing. Today, it's been nothing but total crap. And yes, it obviously must have come as a shock that I'd envisioned Sierra, whose parents had bred her for Harvard, walking to Physics 101 on the Middlesex Community College campus, but it's not my fault. I just deliver the mail; I don't write it.

"Are you . . . su-ure?" she asks me, sniffling and wiping her nose with the back of her hand.

I sigh. This is the inevitable question, and I always answer the same thing: "I'm sorry, but I've never been wrong."

I know that probably makes me sound like a total snob, but it's simple fact. Since freshman year, I've correctly predicted the futures of dozens of students at Stevens. It all started way before that, though, in junior high, when I correctly guessed who would win the million-dollar prize on every reality-TV show out there. At times I would have to think, really think, to know the answer, but sometimes I would just wake up and, clear as day, the face of the winner would pop into my mind. Soon, I started testing my abilities out on my friends, and my friends' friends, and before long, every other person at school wanted my services. Seriously, being a psychic will do more for your reputation than a driver's license or a head-to-toe Marc Jacobs wardrobe.

Sierra tosses her frizzed-out, corn-husk-blond spirals over her shoulder and straightens. "Well, maybe you saw someone else. Someone who looked like me. Isn't that possible?"

Actually, it isn't possible at all. Sierra has a totally warped sense of style, like Andy Warhol on crack. Everyday things lying around the house do not always make attractive accessories. I shrug, though, since I don't feel like explaining that hell would have a ski resort before two people on the face of this earth would think it was okay to tie their ponytail up in a Twizzler, and crane my neck toward the refreshment stand. I'm starving. Where are my French fries?

"I mean, I did get a twenty-three hundred on my SATs," she says, which is something she's told me, and the rest of the student body, about a billion times. She might as well have broadcast it on CNN. However, she hasn't taken into account the fact that there are thousands of other students across the country who also got those scores, and took college-level physics or calculus instead of Dramatic Expression as their senior extracurricular activity. Everyone knows that Sierra Martin screwed herself by deciding to coast through her classes this year.

See, I'm not *that* spooky. Truth is, most people don't use enough of their brains to see the obvious. Part of it is just being keenly aware of human nature, like one of those British detectives on PBS. It's elementary, my dear Watson. Colonel Mustard in the Billiard Room with the candlestick, and Sierra is *so* not Harvard material.

"We need to do the wave," Eden says, grabbing my arm. She doesn't bother to look at me; her attention is focused totally on the game, as usual. "They need us."

I squint at her. "It's an exhibition game."

She pulls a half-sucked Blow Pop from her mouth with a smack and says, "So?"

"Okay, you go, girl," I say, though I wish she wouldn't.

She turns around to face the dozen or so students in the bleachers, cups her hands around her lips, and screams, "Okay, let's do the wave!" Auburn hair trailing like a comet's tail, she runs as fast as her skinny, freckled legs can carry her to the right edge of the seats, then flails her arms and says to the handful of people there, "You guys first. Ready? One, and two, and three, and *go!*"

I don't bother to turn around. I know nobody is doing it. It's human nature—doing a wave during an exhibition game is totally lame. Actually, doing a wave at all is totally lame. And nobody is going to listen to poor Miss Didn't-Make-the-Cheerleading-Squad.

She scowls and screams, "Morgan!" as she rushes past me, so I feel compelled to half stand. I raise my hands a little and let out a "woo!" Sierra doesn't notice Eden's fit of school spirit, since she's still babbling on about her three years as editor of the yearbook, as if giving me her entire life story will somehow get her closer to the Ivy League.

Eden returns a few seconds later, defeated, and slumps beside me. The spray of freckles on her face has completely disappeared into the deep crevasse on the bridge of her nose. "This school has no spirit."

It's true—and ironic, really—that, though my best friend, Eden McCarthy, probably has more school spirit in her pinky than the entire student body put together, she didn't make cheerleading. Being a cheerleader, though, isn't just about having spirit.

Eden could make a cow look graceful. I say, "Well, good try; *A* for effort," and pat her back.

"But, *Morgan,*" she whines, "it's Cameron out there. He's about to score another touchdown."

For the first time in a half hour, I look toward the field. And, wouldn't you know it, the Hawks are on the ten-yard line. I watch as the ball is hiked into the hands of my boyfriend, Cameron Browne. He backs up on the toes of his Nike cleats and throws the ball perfectly to the wide receiver, who is tackled at the one. "Oh. Good."

"You could try being a little more supportive," Eden says with a sigh.

"But you have enough school spirit for the both of us," I say, giving her a hug, even though I'm kind of irked by the insinuation. Of course I support Cam. Otherwise I wouldn't have spent every Saturday night in October last year with my butt frozen to the bleachers, sipping watery hot cocoa and watching my manicure turn all shades of purple. "And it's just an exhibition game."

Anyway, if you know Cam, which I do, since we've been attached at the hip since kindergarten, you know that he does not need a cheering audience in order to kick ass. He's incredible, which is why he's the only sophomore on the varsity football team. In fact, the Sunday *Star-Ledger* once said, and I quote, "It appears that Cam Browne can do anything."

And, ahem, he's all mine.

"That's my boy!" I shout out, mainly to appease Eden, and give him a wolf whistle. Few girls can wolf-whistle like I can, but that's because I've had so much practice. Because Cam Browne "can do anything." And everything he does seems to deserve one. He turns, grins, then holds up three fingers, brings them to his mouth, and points them at me. One, two, three. That's our secret way of saying "I love you." Since we were together when other kids from our class were still in the "Ew! Cooties!" stage, we learned to keep everything corny and romantic a secret. Back then, our lives depended on it. Now, it's habit.

"First and ten. Do it again!" Eden shouts another one of the Hawkettes' most popular cheers. She knows them all by heart. Luckily, she doesn't do the arm movements, or else I don't think I could be seen with her.

Sierra must have realized I'm not listening to her. She clears her throat. "I know you don't care, but this is *important.*"

That's the worst part about being psychic to high-schoolers; they're so insecure. You can't just be the all-knowing prophet who spits out wise fortune-cookie sayings all day—you have to be part "Dear Abby," too. "I do care, Si. I feel really bad for you, honest. But you have to move on. Rise above it."

"Easy for you to say. You probably already saw yourself at Yale," she says bitterly.

I shake my head. "I'm not very good at seeing my own future."

It's kind of like being a genie; I have this amazing power, and yet I can't use it on myself. But I'm okay with that. I'm only a sophomore, so, though my college choice is pretty much up in the air, it's probably the only thing that is. I know that my future is with Cam. I know he and I will go to the same school, or at least schools close to one another. After all, we're next-door neighbors, and we've known each other almost since we could walk. We'll both be turning sixteen on October 15. We're so in

{6}

tune with one another that I can detect when he's having a bad day from a football field's length away.

But Cam rarely has bad days. Today, as usual, he's in top form.

"Be. Aggressive. Be. More. Aggressive. B-E A-G-G-R-E-S-S-I-V-E!" Eden shouts as Sara Phillips, an actual cheerleader, walks past and rolls her eyes.

Eden doesn't seem to notice. She is clueless in so many ways, which makes her my polar opposite. For example, she has had a crush on Mike Kensington forever and can't seem to get it through her head that he's obviously gay. His sense of style, the fact that he spends way too much time on his hair . . . none of this has thrown her off, and I refuse to disrupt her plans to one day bear his children. She clutches my arm and screws her eyes shut as Cam shouts, "Hike!"

"Oh, this is so nerve-racking! I can't look!"

I've loved Eden almost as long as I have Cam, but not only is she clumsy and clue challenged, she's also so neurotic that I'm surprised I haven't envisioned her having a heart attack at eighteen. Her grip is enough to cause nerve damage, so I pry her fingers up one by one and say, very calmly, "It's. Just. An. Exhi—"

And that's when it happens.

Cam has the ball in his hands, and he's searching for a receiver, but they're all blocked. A defenseman breaks free from his left and rushes in for the sack. Just as he's about to throw his hands on Cam's shoulders, my boyfriend takes three quick steps forward, and before he can step on the head of a fallen teammate, he's airborne. He sails, like a feather on the wind, over the massive pile of bodies in his way, right into the end zone.

Instantly, the bleachers erupt into thunderous applause, which

{7}

is weird, considering the effect of Eden's recent Wave Effort. Even Sierra jumps to her feet, her bleak future forgotten for the moment.

Eden opens her eyes and shrieks like a banshee. "Oh! He is so amazing!"

I can't move, can't even bring my hands together for applause. I think even my breathing stops, for the moment. Am I the only one who noticed something strange about that last play?

Am I nuts, or did my boyfriend just *fly*?

MAYBE OUR NEWSPAPER is right. Cam Browne really *can* do anything.

The Hawks win the game, which sends Eden into a state of euphoria I thought could only be achieved by doing meth. Even if it's just an exhibition game. And, hello? The win was no surprise. Her best friend is a psychic, after all.

Following every win, we go to the Parsonage Diner and the boys eat. A lot. I get a celebratory chocolate milk shake. I'd never thought there was such a thing as too much chocolate, but last year, I had so many milk shakes that now I can't look at one without getting a little queasy.

This year, the J. P. Stevens Hawks will probably be New Jersey's finest again, though I haven't actually envisioned that.

My gift can be a little tricky to control sometimes, because I never know exactly to *when* in the future it's going to take me. Plus, Cam doesn't want to know. He's one of those "let the chips fall where they may" types.

After twirling my hair into a ponytail in the lav, I spot Cam at a booth, and immediately I catch my breath. When he's scrubbed up like that, his broad chest pressed solid against his T-shirt, shoots of black hair falling carelessly into his cavernous brown eyes, he can still make my heart flutter. I'd like to say that, lookswise, I'm just as showstopping, but aside from my psychic abilities, there isn't anything remarkable about me. So, though we've been together this long, the phrase "Is he really mine?" always seems to repeat in my mind like a broken record. He's using some foreign football language with Scab and the other maniacs on the team that mostly includes a series of grunts and growls, so I part the sea of testosterone by sliding in next to him and giving him a kiss. "Just as I predicted," I tease.

He takes a crinkled envelope with today's date on it out of the back pocket of his jeans and tears it open with his teeth. Pulling out a slip of paper, he reads to the table, 'Twenty-four to seven, Hawks.' Morgan wins again."

I grin proudly as the rest of the guys congratulate me on another correct prediction. This time, it's even more halfhearted than it was last weekend. Sigh. My powers impressed them like crazy my freshman year, but the effect must be wearing off. When I complained to Cam last week about how nobody really appreciates my gift anymore, he suggested that maybe they still would if I gave them the predictions in my underwear.

Eden stares at my boyfriend dreamily. She says to him, "That touchdown in the second quarter was a*maz*ing."

That was when he'd done the Superman.

The thing I love most about Cam is that, though the entire warped little microcosm that is Stevens High adores him, he remains humble and shy. He blushes and says, "Well, thanks."

"Yeah," I add, "you practically flew."

Cam turns to me for a second, a dazed expression on his face, then nudges Scab. "Scab put that play together."

Scab, Cam's best friend, fits the football-player mold perfectly. When we were younger, he used to pick all his mosquito bites until he was just one big, bleeding sore. Now, he has a round, ruddy face, and he's bigger than a Mack truck and rough around the edges. The nickname, strangely, has always suited him. He polishes off a superdeluxe breakfast with sausage, bacon, eggs, and a double stack of pancakes, punches Cam on the shoulder, and laughs like a chain-smoker, a kind of "haw haw haw." There's a red ring of ketchup, like lipstick, on his mouth. Blech.

Just then, Sara Phillips prances by in her cheerleading outfit. Eden calls, "Great job, Sara!" to her, since she's still holding out hope that the squad will give her a place junior year. Scab gives her a ketchup-soaked grin, and she waves and says sweetly, "Hi, Marcus!" He is so infatuated, and has been forever. At this point, it's kind of a joke.

He turns to Cam and says under his breath, "She totally wants me."

Cam and I look at each other, then burst out laughing.

"What? She's just playing hard to get."

"Since kindergarten?" Cam asks.

Scab comes to me for defense. "Hey, Morg. Don't any of your visions show us together? You saw the way she looked at me."

I pass him a napkin. "Maybe she was jealous of your lipstick."

Dejected, he wipes his mouth and shakes his head.

"Besides," I say, "I told you, I see you playing defense at some college with palm trees."

That perks him right up. "Miami, baby!"

And they all start growling and high-fiving again. Blech.

Eden starts talking to John Vaughn, who is safety. He's really cute and nice, and I think they'd make a great couple, which means they'll never get together. I, unfortunately, envision Eden being thirty and living in a cramped apartment with nobody but fourteen cats and a collection of Precious Moments figurines to talk to. Especially since she doesn't seem likely to figure out that her major crush is playing for the other team anytime this century. John, who so blatantly has a thing for Eden that he might as well print up T-shirts advertising the fact, says to her, "It's cool you come to all the games and practices."

Eden says, "School spirit is important. Last year's championship game was, like, the greatest night of my life. It was so fun."

I elbow her. "Ahem. Well, I hope that will change next Friday."

She thinks for a second and then shrugs. "Oh, right. I can't wait."

"My sweet sixteen," I explain to John. "Next Friday, October fifteenth. It's going to be really big."

He raises his eyebrows. For some reason, guys just don't get the whole sweet-sixteen thing. But mine is going to be one big-with-a-capital-*B* party. Not like a Super Sweet Sixteen on MTV (my parents aren't owners of a rap label or anything), but pretty cool, since my father was college roommates with the manager of the Green Toad, a very exclusive restaurant in the city. I've been planning the event since April, and it's all Eden and I ever talk about now.

John doesn't feel the excitement. "Sounds cool."

"It's at the Toad!" Eden exclaims.

"You're invited," I say. "Didn't you get the invite?"

He looks confused. "Uh, I don't know."

Huh. Boys. Whatever; it's still going to be fantastic. "It's actually a joint birthday party for me and Cam, since we're both turning sixteen," I tell him, nudging Cam, who is busy flicking through the pages of music on the tabletop jukebox at our booth. "Right?"

Cam looks at me. "Huh?"

"I was just talking about our birthday," I tell him.

"What about it?"

Hello? Earth to Cam. "Our sweet sixteen?"

He purses his lips, hesitates, and then says, "Oh. Yeah." Then he goes back to flipping through the music.

Huh. Totally not the response I was expecting. Last year, when I brought up the idea, he was into it. He said he couldn't wait to put on a fancy suit and have a really swanky night, just like a prom. Maybe the guys got to him. I mean, wanting to have a sweet sixteen isn't exactly something a football player would admit to.

"What's wrong?" I say, shaking him by the elbow. I wrap my arm around him and lean in close. He smells clean, like soap and his barbershop aftershave. "You okay?"

He shrugs, then relaxes. "It may be a sweet sixteen for you, but for me, it's a studly sixteen." He says this with a deep, sexy voice and, though I'm not sure how he manages it, a completely straight face. Then he breaks into a grin.

The other guys laugh and I roll my eyes. "Oh, excuse me."

Abruptly, his smile disappears, and he shuffles in his seat. "Hey, I've got to get up."

"What's—" I begin, but he slides out of the booth and scrambles past the dessert case before I have a chance to get the "up?" part out. Okay, so maybe he just had a major urge to pee or something.

Scab and the guys begin to go on about the plans for their next game. At least, I think that's what they're doing, because this is what I hear: "Blabbity blah blah blah." It's so boring, I'm superaware of every passing second that Cam is gone. And we're talking many, many seconds. After roughly fifteen hundred of them, I begin to wonder whether terrorists hijacked his urinal.

By the time the guys start to write plays on the backs of napkins, I've had enough. I take another sip of my milk shake, stand up, and navigate around the dessert case, toward the restrooms. I'm halfway there, at the cash register near the entrance, when I look into the front vestibule and see Cam. He's standing among the nickel-candy dispensers and free-newspaper racks. He has his hands shoved in his pockets and is surveying a bulletin board filled with want ads. He's staring intently at one that says 25' SCHOONER FOR SALE.

What is going on? Does he suddenly want to become the Skipper?

I open my mouth to say something to him, but before I can, he turns, grabs my hand, and looks intently at me. "You saw it, didn't you? That play?"

"Yeah." The intensity in his eyes makes the hair on the back of my neck stand on end. "It was amazing. So?"

"Everyone keeps saying that, Boo," he says, using his way-embarrassing nickname for me. In first grade I was a child of few words. One, actually. I found that not only could it be used as a frightening tactic, but it was also extremely effective as a question, a statement, a cry of frustration. Yes, I was weird. Leave it to Cam to bring up my long-lost weirdness on a daily basis.

"Because it was. Just accept it. Would you like me to feed you grapes?"

He glares at me.

"Sorry. What's the big deal? You should be happy."

He exhales slowly. "I probably would be. If I could remember any of it."

MY PARENTS THINK they're so smart. Every time I go out with Cam, the porch furniture miraculously moves three feet away from the side of the house, so I nearly trip over it when I come home. As most concerned parents would, they leave the light on, but they also arrange the metal glider and side table so that they are in perfect view from the garage window. My dad has maintained a stalwart post from that window for so long that he might as well set up a Barcalounger and minifridge there. He thinks Cam and I don't know, despite the way the curtain in the window does nothing to disguise his hefty silhouette, and the way he says his good nights—completely out of breath after hightailing all four hundred pounds of his flesh up the stairs before I can get inside. Once, in the early days, I went into the garage at 11 p.m. to find him "fixing the lawn mower." Cam had the bright idea a few years back of using the situation to our advantage instead of busting him, which would be way uncomfortable.

And it would have worked great if only Cam weren't the worst liar in the world.

"Wow, it's fifteen minutes past your curfew, Morg," Cam says in this loud voice as we settle onto the swing. "If only you hadn't Heimliched that poor old lady who was choking on the meat loaf, we would have been home from our volunteer work at the soup kitchen on time."

"Yes!" I say, then shake my head at him and whisper, "I love you, but you really suck at this." My dad can't possibly believe that I work at the soup kitchen, the ASPCA, the League of Women Voters, and Greenpeace.

Cam grabs me longingly, like he's going to launch into the steamiest hookup since *The Notebook,* and then, when my face is an inch from his, gives me a very sterile, grandmotherly peck on the cheek. "Sorry."

At times like this, the "Is he really mine?" recording plays loudest in my head. He has the sexy bad-boy face, with dark skin, the black, intense eyes of an animal on the hunt, and, since last year, a constant spray of stubble on his jaw. That alone makes him easily the hottest guy at school, but he's also got a wicked sense of humor. And, to seal the deal, he's a total sweetie. My long, sometimes frizzy chestnut hair; heavy, dull brown eyes; pale complexion; strong profile, with what my father calls a pronounced but I call a freakishly big nose; and body, on the slender side but soft around the edges, make me just average; I've inherited my mother's Sicilian looks. But we

{17}

met when making friends was easy and appearances didn't matter. If we hadn't known each other all these years, I doubt he would have given me a second look.

"So," I whisper, putting my feet up and resting my back against his enormous shoulder, "you don't remember it, really? Like amnesia?"

He shrugs and wraps his arm around me. "I remember the huddle. The next thing I knew, I was flat on my back and the refs were peeling guys off me."

"You must have gotten hit pretty hard," I tell him, matching my palm against his. His hands are twice the size of mine, and I can feel the calluses beneath each finger from his daily weightlifting sessions. "You'll be fine."

"But I've never blacked out like that before."

Boys. Such babies. I push my back against him. He's two of me, so it's like trying to move Mount Everest. "Is there anything, other than your ass, you want me to kiss and make better?"

He smiles and pats his backside. "You can't improve on this perfection."

I try to smack him, but he grabs my wrist and leans over me to kiss me. He gets the bottom of my cheek, right near the tip of my chin, instead of my mouth. Huh. Missing the mark is totally uncharacteristic of Cam. "Hey. It's nothing. Don't let it get to you," I growl at him.

"I'm not. I'm just tired," he says.

"Okay, if you say so." Did I mention that Cam is a terrible liar?

He leans over to kiss me on the forehead, slides his body out from behind me, and stands. Then he loudly says, "I hope to see you tomorrow, for our UNICEF meeting."

"Whatever," I sigh as he turns and heads off between two manicured bushes surrounding my porch. Cutting across my lawn is the quickest way to his house. There's a little path worn into the grass there; we've involuntarily created it after years of visiting each other. We could both walk that route in our sleep.

I hear my father lumbering up the stairs inside my house. I decide to give the old man a minute's head start, so I sit back, watching a moth dance in the porch light. I'm expecting to hear the creaking of the Brownes' screen door, but it never comes.

I stand up and walk to the edge of the porch. It's getting chilly, so I pull my jacket around my shoulders and push aside the branch of a Japanese maple that's resting on the railing. That's when I see Cam standing all alone, staring up at the sky.

I knew it. He's letting it get to him.

AFTER A HEARTY Neutrogena scrubbing and my daily application of Whitestrips (one's teeth can never be too straight or too white), I turn off my bedside lamp and slide under the covers. Moonlight slashes through my window and the open shades, painting a tic-tac-toe board on the wall. Cam's bedroom is across from mine, and, though his heavy curtains are drawn, they're rimmed in yellow light. He's still awake. This, from a guy who has been known to fall asleep at the dinner table.

I quickly pick up the phone and dial his number. Before he can call out a greeting, I say, "Go to sleep."

He laughs, and two seconds later, the curtain pulls back, and he appears in the window. His face is darkened, but I can tell he has his shirt off. Yum. "Stop spying on me."

"Just wanted to catch a glimpse of those rockin' abs of yours," I say. "Ooh, baby."

He starts flexing his muscles like a bodybuilder, giving me a private show. If my parents weren't on the other side of the house, I'd be nervous. Then I see him flop down on his bed, next to his laptop. "I'm fine. Just wound up from the game. Probably going to surf the porn sites now, maybe get myself a mail-order bride."

"Have fun with that." I scrunch the phone between my ear and my shoulder, then pull my dark hair into a ponytail. That's the bad thing about Cam's sense of humor; he's always disguising his worries with one-liners. "On second thought, go to bed. You can be such the ogre when you don't get enough sleep."

He growls into the phone, which makes me laugh. "Okay, Boo. In a sec. One, two, three."

"One, two, three," I say back, pulling the sheet up to my chin and flipping the phone closed.

He jumps up and closes the curtains again, but after that, the light doesn't go off. After another minute of lying on my side, silently willing the room to go dark, I throw off the covers and pull myself up on my elbows. This calls for desperate measures. Cam might not want to know his future, but it doesn't mean that I can't take my own little sneak peek. Just because he blacked out once doesn't mean he's destined to be the subject of the next episode of *House*. Maybe I can find something that will calm him down.

And, okay, me too.

I stumble over the jeans I'd left balled up on the shag rug, grab my iPod, and tune it to some Enya. Then I sit cross-legged on my bed and begin the routine I use to calm myself and help bring up my visions.

Closing my eyes, I picture water. Clear, aquamarine ripples from a swimming pool. I guess I could use any soothing background as a canvas, but a swimming pool is what I've always used. Then I say "Fluffernutter" over and over again, until the syllables fall atop one another. Really, any word or phrase would probably do; it's just something to clear the mind. Just at the time that "Fluffernutter" becomes "lufferfutter," I introduce the name of the subject whose future I want to see. After two or three minutes, the waves become grainy, and images begin to float up to the surface. Fuzzy at first, they eventually clear, and I can see the subject just like they're on TV. I've predicted so many futures that I've found this method works best for me. But I still haven't gotten all the kinks out. For one thing, there's no sound in my visions. I can't hear what people are saying. And, even worse, I can't control what point in the future my gift will take me to. It might be tomorrow, or it might be fifty years from now. Sometimes I can scan the surroundings to catch a sign or something in the background, but not always.

"Lufferfluffernuffer . . . ," I say, massaging my temples and staring at the cool, inviting water. "Show me Cam Browne."

The image of Cam's face floats up. He's sitting on the corner of a stool, hunched over, elbows on his knees. Completely normal—that is, until I see the look on his face. It looks like he swallowed ammonia. In fifteen years I'd never realized Cam's sexy facial muscles had such flexibility to contort into something that hideous. A chill pecks at my shoulders. What could be so wrong?

The camera pans back, and then I see he's surrounded by art. The most horrendous paintings I've ever seen. Where is he—the Academy of Fine Arts for the Blind? And Cam has his T-shirt pulled up to his armpits. Then I see myself, standing behind him. What am I doing? Giving him a massage? Like that would ever happen.

That's when I notice my expression. It's like I just saw my grandfather naked. I'm staring at his back and clearly disgusted. And . . . are those tears in my eyes? I admit to being a bit of a leaky faucet, but Cam's muscular back, with the way it comes to a perfect V over his tight waist, usually makes me drool like a dog. So what about it could have reduced me to crying? A mongo-zit?

I scrunch my nose and find myself snapping my head over, willing myself to switch viewpoints, to pan behind his shoulder so I can see what's up. That's another bad thing about my gift. I have absolutely no control over what I can or can't see. Someone else is holding the camera, so at times it has a way of showing enough to pique my curiosity, but not the whole story. I found it merely annoying when it showed Emily Andersen convulsing at the sight of her PSAT scores yet wouldn't show actual numbers, but this is unbearable.

The vision pops out of my head, so I pull my earphones down and open my eyes. Tossing my iPod aside, I bear-hug my pillow and turn toward the window. Cam's light is still on. I imagine telling Cam tomorrow, "Don't worry, hon. I may not have discovered why you blacked out at the game yesterday, but I did find out that you will soon be the proud owner of a gross back pimple. Now, doesn't that make you feel better?"

I'm nearly asleep by the time it hits me. I sit up straight in bed, and my entire body goes cold.

I FLIP ON the lights and call Eden on my cell. "Cam is dying," I cry out, before she even says hello.

"Wha. . . ?" a half-human voice comes back.

"Wake up. Did you hear me?"

"Yeah, but . . ." A long groan. "It's two in the morning!"

I can't breathe, because my heart is in my throat and it's cutting off my oxygen supply. "Did you hear me? He's dying. *Dying*."

"To do what?"

"Eden! I mean death. Skull and crossbones. Big scary dude with a sickle. He's sick."

With that, I start to cry, big, sloppy tears that run down my chin and schmutz up my Neutrogena facial.

"What do you mean, sick?"

"Cam blacked out during the game," I tell her. "It's a tumor."

"What? Oh, my God. But he was fine a few hours ago. He did that a*maz*ing play." She sounds like she might cry, too. Finally, the reaction I was looking for.

"I know. What am I going to do? I saw it on an episode of *ER* once. This awesomely talented figure skater was having blackouts and seizures, and it turned out that she had a tumor in her spine."

"How did he find out? Did he go to the doctor?"

I pick up the corner of my pink sheet and run it over my eyes. I stop short of using it to blow my nose. "He doesn't know."

"You mean . . ." There's this extended pause. The elevator might not always go to Eden's top floor, but she's been friends with me long enough to get the picture. She makes a clucking noise with her tongue. "Don't tell me . . . you didn't . . . What exactly did you see?"

"He had his shirt off. I was looking at his back . . . and it was horrible. I couldn't see exactly what it was I was looking at, but I was *crying*."

"You cried when they canceled *The OC*," she points out. "It could be heat rash. That stuff is nasty."

"But then, why did he black out today?"

"I don't know. God, Morg, you are the worst psychic ever. You're like a TV that only gets local channels."

I'd be hurt, but Eden has good reason to think that. Every time I try to look into her future, I see her in the apartment, alone, talking to her Precious Moments figurines. I'd hate to tell her that, so when she asks me to tell her future, I usually reveal something obvious, like, "You will be eating pizza for dinner tomorrow," which is a given, because her father has no culinary skills.

{25}

"Anyway, I have my own problems." She sighs. "Mike called me."

I can sense the excitement in her voice, which is so sad, considering how the only way he'd ever call her for the reasons she's hoping would be if she sprouted testicles and chest hair overnight. "He did? For what?"

"I have no idea. I missed the call because I was doing my Whitestrips," she whines. She and I have a matching obsession for white teeth. "I can't believe it. He finally calls me, and I miss the freaking call."

"Did he leave a message?"

"No! Can you believe it?" She cries in a voice that makes me wonder if prior to my call, she wasn't trying to hang herself with her bedsheets. "I think, maybe, it was, like, a social call."

I'm not betting on it, but she sounds so hopeful. "Possibly," I say. "So call him back and find out."

"No, I don't want him to think I'm the type of girl who spends hours analyzing her missed calls. That would look totally desperate, don't you think?"

"Okay, okay. So just keep your phone glued to your side for the next time he calls."

"What if he never calls?"

She goes on about how she thinks he wants to ask her out but is just too shy and how the birthmark on his upper cheek is just so wonderful and blah blah blah.

"What if he dies and leaves me alone?" I ask, finally breaking into part 3 of the dream she had about Mike last night, in which they were floating about on a polar ice cap, having a snowball fight. I am not sure what makes people think that others want to hear their dreams, but can anything possibly be more boring?

"Who?" she asks, temporarily confused. "Cam? You two are going to be together forever."

"That's what I thought." I sigh, thinking of the girls at school. Most of them are going through hell for guys—playing weird head games like "ignore him and he'll fall all over you" or seeing who can fit into the clothes with the biggest price tags and the smallest sizes. I've never been a part of that world, and I don't want to be. I want to be with Cam. That's the only thing about my life that makes sense.

Then I turn toward my bedside table, where there's a picture of Cam and me on the Kingda Ka roller coaster, from a day trip we took to Six Flags Great Adventure last summer. He has his arms up straight over his head in victory; I have my eyes clamped tightly shut, and I'm squeezed so close to him, they could have fit another person in the seat with me. My face is twisted in agony. Though I'd begged him not to buy it, since I look like hell, Cam did anyway, "because," he'd said, "even though you thought you'd die, you survived. And you need to remember that. Things aren't as bad as they seem."

Things aren't as bad as they seem, I repeat to myself.

Meanwhile, Eden is going on. "Stop it. He's not dying."

I catch my reflection in the mirror across the room and notice my bugged-out, unfocused eyes. I'm acting like a total loser. "I'm not thinking straight. I'm probably getting all worked up over something a tube of calamine lotion can fix. I'm just tired."

"What do you think it means?" she asks.

"I don't know . . ." In the mirror, I can see the tips of my fingers turning white on my cell phone, and it's only then that I realize I'm holding it in a sweaty death grip. "I guess it could be heat rash."

"I was talking about my dream. I mean, polar ice caps? Where do you think *that* came from? Totally odd."

"Oh. Um." I know exactly what it means, actually. That she has a snowball's chance in hell of ever heating anything up with Mike Kensington. Even her subconscious is more informed than she is. "Maybe that you're two cold, lonely souls searching for love?"

The line is silent as she contemplates that load of crap for a moment. "Yeah. That could be. Do you think you could . . ."

I know what she's asking. It's the way most people start conversations with me: "Do you think you could tell my future?" "Sure, one sec," I say. I put the phone down for a minute, study my nails, the picture of Cam and me on Kingda Ka, a dust bunny skimming across the floor of my room. "Sorry. Pizza again."

"Gah!" she screams. "I know you love me, but your gift hates me."

"Sorry. I do love you, though. And if Mike doesn't, too, he's an idiot. Or . . . gay."

She giggles as if it's the most insane idea in the world. "Night, Morgan."

I press End on the phone and flip it closed, then sink under the covers again. The light is finally out in Cam's bedroom, and somehow, I fall asleep.

M Y PARENTS ARE the world's youngest senior citizens. They have spent virtually every night since I was a kid watching old TV Land reruns in our family room. They dim the lights, which makes it "just like a movie theater," according to my mom, then pop some microwave Orville Redenbacher and sit on their respective matching recliners until they fall asleep. They refuse to go anywhere for dinner unless they have a coupon or know of an early-bird special, and they need to be home before dark, since they're both afraid of driving at night.

Yawn.

That's why I have absolutely no idea how I ended up a psychic. You'd expect someone with such a gift to have parents with equally thrilling abilities, like telekinesis or the power to see through people's clothes. But they've got nada. My dad can say the capitals of the fifty states in alphabetical order, but that's where the magic ends.

"You must be exhausted," my mom, who never gets fewer than ten hours of sleep a night, says after offering me a glass of OJ.

I can tell she's fishing for something. "Not really. And before you go asking, I did my homework in study hall."

Scissors in hand, she looks up from a stack of advertisements and several piles of coupons, which she has sorted by supermarket aisle. "I wasn't saying anything," she says defensively.

"Ri-ight."

"Any plans for the weekend?" she asks casually, even though I'm sure she's dying to know so that she can arrange the porch furniture accordingly.

"Not sure yet," I tell her. Though I'd eventually made it to sleep last night, when morning came, a new batch of worries dawned on me: If Cam is sick, I'll have to be the strong one. And who am I kidding—I rely on him to kill spiders in my room the size of my thumbnail. My hair gel is stronger than I am.

"No plans with Cameron?" she asks as I'm shaking the Cheerios box to get the last few Os into my dish.

Ugh. "Mom! I said I'm not sure."

She raises her hands in surrender. "Excuse me for caring. I want to know if I can expect you home for dinner at all. I'm making *sfogliatelle* for the Nelsons, and you know how they dirty up the kitchen."

Uh-oh. My mother only whips up her *sfogliatelle* when there's an impending death. A hundred years ago, one of her great-great-grandfathers was on his deathbed in Italy, and it was his wife's famous *sfogliatelle* recipe that brought him back from the

{30}

beyond. He was able to live another ten healthy years, until he fell into a well. Or something like that. So, though they haven't saved a person since, the recipe has been part of a sacred, treasured family tradition. Italians are weird like that. "Who's dying?"

My mother grasps for her heart. "Oh, it's terrible. Their little daughter, Gracie." She whispers, "Leukemia. She isn't supposed to last the month."

"Oh," I say, realizing I haven't seen the little blond, pigtailed girl tricycling on the sidewalk opposite us in a while. "That's so sad."

My mother nods and continues to clip a coupon for twenty cents off fabric-softener sheets. "Are the Brownes having company? I saw a young man there."

Thank God my parents have no clue about my psychic abilities, or else they'd probably have me envisioning the futures of half the residents of Oak Court, which, considering the number of geriatrics on this street, would be enough to put me into a coma. I contemplate taking my breakfast somewhere far, far away, like Pluto, but I know we'll just end up yelling the rest of the conversation to one another from our respective planets. I reluctantly pull up the chair across from her and say, "What young man?"

"He was very handsome," she says reflectively.

"Um, are you sure it wasn't Cam?"

"It was a blond boy."

I shrug. "Maybe it was someone selling Bibles or something."

She thinks for a moment. "Well, he did have a suitcase. But I saw them in their backyard, drinking iced tea, and Ingrid had her arm around him. She seemed rather agitated."

Oooh, drama. "Is Mrs. Browne having an affair?" I say, raising my eyebrows. "With a younger guy? Sweet."

{31}

My mom shoots me a disapproving look. "Mr. Browne was there, too."

"Oh." My interest plummets. "Maybe they're adopting a Scandinavian orphan?"

She sighs. "Well, maybe you can ask Cameron when you see him next. I would invite Ingrid over for coffee if I thought it would do anything, but she's so tight-lipped."

Smart woman, I think. I like the Brownes. In a way, they're just like Cam . . . perfect. In all the years we've lived next door to each other, they've been model neighbors. I've never seen so much as a maxi-pad wrapper sticking out from their garbage or heard the slightest noise from an argument wafting over the picket fence separating our backyards.

I'm glad when my cell phone rings, interrupting the conversation. When I check the display and see Cam's name, my heart jumps into my throat. I flip it open and say, in my sweetest voice, "Hi, baby."

"Hey."

The gruffness of his voice startles me. Total Mr. Grouchy Pants.

"How are you? Do you feel okay today?"

"Yeah. Listen, I can't walk with you today. I've got something to take care of before school." His voice is so serious that the pile of worry I'd just buried quickly resurfaces.

I try to remain calm. "Oh, sure. What?"

"Can we talk about it later?" He sounds rushed.

"Um, yeah. But, Cam . . ." Should I tell him? Should I say that I know about the tumor? Or should I just let him go? I'm not sure if I would be able to stem the tide of tears and snot before they shorted out my cell phone.

As I'm contemplating, his voice comes across, rough: "What?"

"Are you okay?" My voice is a squeak.

"I said I was fine."

"But you are a terrible liar."

He laughs, a short, hardly-there laugh. "Can't you just let me pick up my mail-order bride at the post office in peace?"

There he goes again, using humor as a disguise. Though it helps to ease the tension a bit, I can't bring myself to laugh.

"Okay. One, two—" I begin, but the line goes dead. I pull the phone away from my ear and see Call Ended flashing, taunting me.

I<small>F</small> I'<small>D</small> <small>HAD</small> someone other than Tanner for geometry, maybe I could have gotten away with it. If it had been later in the year, maybe Tanner would have understood that being late is so not me. Or maybe he would have been so awed by my mathematical capabilities that he would have let me slide. But Tanner didn't get the nickname Beast for nothing, and, since we're barely out of September, I haven't had enough face time to secure the place in his heart as teacher's pet. I hung my head in abject remorse and tried to explain to him that my locker was stuck, that it would never happen again, et cetera, et cetera, but he continued to scribble out the pink slip. When he ripped it from the pad and handed it to me, I tried to ask him where I needed to report, in hopes that I'd subtly get him to realize that

I'd never gotten a tardy slip before, that this was all just a huge mistake and he was tarnishing the record of a possible future nuclear physicist. But I stopped midsentence, since his eyes were so demonic that I was surprised his head didn't do a 360.

Now I'm sitting in the front office, with a bald Goth girl in a Kill Your Mother T-shirt and a dude who appears to have forgotten to wear his pants today, since he's just wearing white boxers. Despite their obvious problems, the bunch of ancient women in rhinestone-studded sweatshirts who work in attendance keep inspecting me over their bifocals like I'm a tinfoil-wrapped package found in the back of their freezer. *Me.* I'm probably the only student in the room who doesn't do meth as an extracurricular activity, and yet I get the dirty looks.

"Morgan?" the largest of the three grannies asks, pushing a paper over the counter toward me.

I stand up and take the paper from her.

"You can go back to class. Principal Edwards doesn't want to waste time with you, since this is your first offense. Just don't let it happen again," she growls, with more force than I'd ever have believed an Auntie Em type could muster. If this is how they treat their honors students, I expect Goth Girl and Mr. No-Pants may be thrown into a pit with rabid wolves.

I turn to leave and catch the pantsless guy checking out my legs and making a rude gesture. Which only makes me think of Cam and how if I didn't have him, I would have become a nun years ago. Startled, I drop my geometry book. As I lean over to pick it up, very demurely, so as not to give the psycho a free show, the door to the office opens, and I see a pair of Keds shuffle in, topped by horrible floods that reveal white sweat socks. There's no excuse for that fashion disaster. I scan upward, way, way upward, and see that the fashion faux pas belongs to a basketball-player frame. The disaster isn't just below the knees, though. The cords he's wearing are way too tight in, uh, certain places, and he's wearing a plaid farmer shirt.

"Yo, man, Halloween's like a month away," No-Pants hisses at him. Not like he should talk, but he does have a point. I mean, why else would anyone wear cords from the kids' department and put enough oil in his hair to power a Hummer?

I'm so taken aback by the sight that I lose my balance as I'm straightening and nearly fall headfirst into No-Pants's lap. Luckily, I manage to steady myself.

"Excuse me," I hear the geek say to Auntie Em in a prepubescent voice, "I can't seem to figure this out."

I'm happy when I hear her use the same gruff tone of voice that she used with me. "What? Your locker combination?"

His voice wavers. "Yes. And I am not sure where I am supposed to go. Is it . . . Mr. Tanner?"

I stop at the door and turn to him. "You have Tanner for geometry?"

He turns around, eyes wide. I've scared him. Wiping his nose, he nods, but his eyes never really meet mine.

"That's my class. I can take you," I say, looking over to Auntie Em to make sure she approves. I figure that once she sees I'm the Girl Scout type, she'll feel bad for ever using that harsh tone of voice with me and apologize profusely. But, unfortunately, she just shrugs and waves us off.

I lead him out the door as No-Pants and Goth Girl stare after me like I've just offered to sell my soul to the devil. But it never hurts to be nice, right?

As we walk down the hall, I notice he's not. Walking, I mean. He shuffles, toes pointed outward, like he's sweeping the floor with his sneakers.

Swish, swish, swish. He's like a human Swiffer.

Thank God the hallways are empty, so I don't have to explain why I'm with him. He's clutching a paper bag in his pale hands, and a little red plastic box. Is that a . . . wait. Is that a pencil box? Like the kind we used in first grade? Oh, hell.

"Um, so . . . ," I start as we swish along. "I guess you're new."

I steal a glance at him and realize he's so flushed, you can see the red of his scalp peeking out from between the greased-back shards of hair on his head. "Er, no, I'm fifteen years of age," he says softly.

"I mean, like, new to the school?"

"Ah. Er. Yes. This is my first day at this facility," he says.

Facility? Who refers to a school in the same way they'd refer to a toilet? Huh, he has a point. Still, I'm convinced I saw this guy profiled on *America's Most Wanted* last Sunday. "He was a quiet kid, always kept to himself," they'd said.

I'm holding his locker-assignment slip by one crumpled corner, since it is still kind of—ew—clammy from being in his hands. We pass a hundred aqua-colored doors in the science wing, finally landing at number 1687. "Here you go," I say. I reach over and fiddle with the knob. "See, all you have to do is go fourteen this way, then one full turn to twenty-eight, and then back this way to zero. Simple."

He watches, completely perplexed, as I lift the handle and the door swings open. "I see," he mumbles, and it's obvious that he doesn't.

I demonstrate the technique another three times and then have him try. He fails on the first attempt but gets the hang of it after I talk him through it.

"Didn't they have lockers in your old school?" I ask, though I'm guessing they must carry their books from class to class on his home planet.

He shakes his head and blushes clear through to his scalp once again. It's kind of cute, in a pitiful way.

"Where are you from?" I ask a generic question, since we have nothing, nothing, nothing, in common. At least, I hope.

"Up north," he answers.

I laugh. "Like, North Jersey . . . or the Arctic?"

"Oh, uh . . . ," he stammers. "The Arctic."

I stare back at him, waiting for him to laugh, to tell me he's just joking. Nothing; total poker face. Fine, I'll play along. "It must be very cold up there."

He nods and closes the locker door. Uh-huh. Fascinating conversation.

I look down at the bag and pencil box in his hands and realize he hasn't put a thing inside. "You want to put your lunch in there?"

"My?" he asks, confused.

I point at the paper bag. "Isn't that your lunch?"

"No, it's my . . ." He pauses just long enough for me to mentally fill in the blank with some scary thoughts: *bodily fluid; severed human head; science experiment ("I'm breeding slugs!")*. Finally, he says, "Yes, it's my lunch," which is a dead giveaway that it's not.

"Don't you want to put it in your locker?"

He shrugs and I again help him to open it. He carefully lays the paper bag on the top shelf, his eyes lingering on it for a moment, and then closes the door.

We walk to the other side of the building in silence because I'm wondering if I could be charged with aiding and abetting for telling him to dispose of his victim's severed head in a locker. Finally, we stop outside the door to Tanner's geometry class.

I figure it's time for a final goodwill gesture, since I plan to never, ever, ever have any contact with this guy again. I extend my hand. "Well, welcome to Stevens."

He looks at it for a moment, then gently takes my fingertips and gives them a little shake, as if he's afraid of catching *my* cooties. "My name is Pip Merriweather."

He says this very properly, like a gay English chap. Pip. Like Pippi Longstocking? What the hell? I search the far corners of my brain to find a normal male name that Pip could possibly be short for and come up with nil.

I contemplate giving a fake name, but he'll figure out the truth anyway, since we're in the same class. Basically, I'm screwed either way. "I'm Morgan. Morgan Sparks."

He turns to me. "I know."

I TRY TO sneak into the room as James Bond–ily as possible, but Mr. Tanner stops his entire lesson. "The area of a parallelo–" is still hanging in the air as I sit at my desk in the back of the classroom. The entire class is staring at me. Tanner's look could melt faces à la the last scene in *Raiders of the Lost Ark,* which is just perfect. I bet I could be Master of Pi from here on out and he'd still want to murder me.

Goofy just stands in the doorway, looking like he wants to bolt. I can see his red scalp shining gloriously from halfway across the room.

Tanner, oblivious, begins again. He booms, "The area of a parallelo–" but is again cut off, this time by Pip's fragile "Ahem?"

Eden sways back and forth in her seat, trying to get a better look, like a second grader who's about to pee her pants. Then she leans over to me. "Is that him?" she whispers, nearly falling out of her seat.

Tanner, a little round man with a dark helmet of hair that makes him so closely resemble a penguin, waddles up to Pip and snatches the paper from his shaky hands.

"Him who?"

"The new kid," she says, as some other people turn and snicker. If they think Pip is snickerworthy now, wait until Tanner announces his name.

I nod as Tanner scowls and motions for Pip, who is now almost convulsing from fear, to sit in an empty seat at the front of the room. "Wait. How did you hear about him?" I ask her.

She looks at me as if I'm a moron. "Uh. From Cam?"

"You saw Cam? Today?"

"Uh-huh."

I'm jealous. But what would Cam have to do with a freak like Pip? "What did he say?" I bark out, much louder than intended.

Tanner, who has been trying to find an extra textbook for his newest student, jerks his head up. "Miss Sparks? See me after class."

Oh hell. Face reddening, I straighten like an exclamation point. This is not my life. I am the student teachers adore, dammit! I give them reason not to go home after a hard day's work and drink themselves into a stupor! I am the one they remember fondly during their retirement dinners!

Eden turns back to me and whispers, "I asked him if he had a spine tumor and he told me you watch too much *ER*."

Tanner waddles back to the front of the classroom and says, "Everyone. This is Pip Merriweather."

A few chuckles. Seriously, though, what would Cam know

about a dude like Pip? I look at Eden, hoping she can communicate the answer telepathically, but she's too busy examining this new specimen of male nerdiness. Most of the eyes in the class are fastened on him as he opens his red plastic box and carefully removes a finely sharpened number 2 pencil, then swipes into place a shock of oiled hair that has fallen over his forehead. I think that hairstyle was maybe in vogue when the Pink Ladies ruled the school.

Tanner turns to a sketch on the blackboard again. He barely gets out "The area of a parallelo–" when the door opens and in walks Scab. He has this very serious look on his face and is staring straight at me. What the . . . ? Then he turns to my teacher and holds out a blue slip of paper. Hell.

Aggravated, Tanner snatches it, reads for a second, and then those demon eyes focus on me. Again.

"Didn't you just come from the principal's office?" he asks accusingly.

Double hell.

I nod, since my vocal cords have frozen up.

"Seems you're wanted there again," he grumbles. I can sort of understand his angst, since he's said "The area of a parallelo–" more than any human should have to in a three-minute period. But what can this be? Principal Edwards changed his mind and now has decided to hang me for being three minutes late? Nobody, not even the legendary Frankie Buzzaro, who didn't graduate until he was twenty-one, gets called to the principal's office twice in one measly half hour! I look at Eden, who shrugs, her eyes wide. My knees go weak as I rise, and one of the guys at the front of the class grins at me and slices his index finger across his throat.

9

BY THE TIME I'm in the hallway, Scab is nowhere in sight. Deserter. I walk toward the office as slowly as possible. There has to be some mistake. Maybe Principal Edwards wants to apologize for Auntie Em's attitude. Maybe they'll feel so horrible for treating me like a felon that they'll give me an award, possibly name a wing of the school after me.

Oh, who am I kidding? I am doomed.

I'm so busy imagining the execution that I don't pay attention when a door swings open. A movement, a blur of red, flashes in my peripheral vision, and I'm snapped into reality when an enormous hand roughly clasps my elbow and jerks me through the doorway of a classroom. As I'm recovering from the jolt and catching my breath, I look up and see Cam.

"What are you—"

He clamps his hand over my mouth. "Shh."

I grab hold of his enormous, sweaty paw and pull it off me. He pulls me into a hug, but his limbs feel stiff. I whisper, "Hey. What is going on?"

"I told you, I had to get some stuff taken care of."

Standing back, I realize he looks terrible. His black hair is uncombed, he's unshaven, and there are rims around his eyes the color of blood.

"Stuff with Pip?"

He exhales deeply and rakes his hands through his hair. "You met him?"

"Yeah. Is he an exchange student from Mars or something?"

He ignores me. "I need your help."

"Okay, I know, I want to talk to you, too." I put my hand on the doorknob. "But I've got to get to the principal's office."

He looks perplexed for a moment, then blocks me from the door. "No, wait. That was me. I had Scab forge a note to get you out."

"You? Thanks for the coronary." I sigh with relief and turn back into the empty room. I realize that I've never been in this classroom; there are easels and stools everywhere, and shelves of paints and art supplies. "What for? You look horrible. Did you shower? Weren't you wearing that shirt yesterday?"

"No, listen. This is serious. I need your help."

I sit down at one of the stools surrounding this enormous wood-topped table, and that's when it hits me. Yes, he was wearing that shirt yesterday.

In my vision.

"Oh, my God," I spit out, surveying the paintings. Yes, they're completely preschool: boring fruit bowls and warped, cartoon-like portraits and landscapes with trees like Popsicle sticks. I mean, yes, my visions are always right. I knew it would happen eventually. I just never thought it would happen so soon. "It's the blackouts, right?"

He nods. He won't look at me.

"The thing on your back?"

His eyes lock with mine. "How long have you known about it?"

"Only since last night." I stand up, position myself behind him, and put my hand on his shoulder. "Does it hurt? Show it to me."

"You don't want to . . ."

"I do."

I expect a joke, something to lighten the mood. Instead, he turns to me, completely serious. Frighteningly so. "No. *I* don't want to."

"Just show it to me," I tell him, with conviction this time.

Don't show him you're worried. Don't let him know how horrible you think it is, I tell myself. Reluctantly, he wraps his big fingers around the bottom edge of his T-shirt and pulls it up, past the ripple of his ribs, over one of his shoulders.

Don't cry, don't scream, I tell myself.

But my visions are always right.

10

"WHAT IS THAT?" I finally say. Dozens of questions are swirling around in my head, but that's the only one I can manage to choke out.

"It's bad, isn't it?" he asks.

"Bad" is an understatement. Just above his shoulder blades, right at his spine, the skin is raised and bumpy, in the shape of an inverted V. His once-tanned, clear back is coated in something waxy, and it all seems to twitch and dance, like it has its own heartbeat. And at the very tip of that V, there's an opening, a small one, a bloody smile. And there's something, a sharp, white sliver, just like a fingernail . . . *poking out.* . . .

I screw my eyes shut and do my best to keep my voice even. "It's not that it's bad, per se. . . . It's just . . ." What is the word for bad to the nineteenth power? Hideous times a million? Even "the most atrocious thing I've ever seen" seems to miss the mark. I mean, last summer, I was addicted to *Untold Stories of the ER* on Discovery Health. I expected, possibly, to see a golf-ball-sized bump under the skin. Maybe a tennis ball. Not *this*. "What the hell is it?"

He—thank God!—pulls his T-shirt down, carefully lowering it over the disgusting, alien growth, and turns to me. He balls his hands into fists and presses firmly down on his thighs, but not before I see his arms quiver. The rock of Stevens, the Cam Browne who can do anything, is trying to steady himself, and that's enough to turn my own knees to Jell-O. When he speaks, his voice is mouselike. "How much did you see in your vision?"

"Just this. What happened right now. That's it." I move around him and put a reassuring hand on his shoulder. "Did you go to the doctor? I can go with you, if you want."

"Doctor?" He shakes his head. "So you didn't see anything else?"

"Um, no. You *are* going to the doctor, aren't you? I mean, I don't think Ben-Gay has the answer to this one."

"So you don't know about her?"

"The doctor?"

"No. *Her*," he says forcefully, then looks around, inspecting the corners of the room, until I'm sure that the hit he endured during last night's game must have shaken more than a screw or two loose.

"Her who?" My voice rises to match his. "Is it a tumor or what?"

"No, it's not." He rakes his fingers through his hair again. "Forget it."

{47}

"No way. I've never seen you this freaked. Who are you talking about?"

The bell rings. In the hall, doors burst open and stampeding students fill every space. Despite the tongue-lashing I received from Tanner and the knowledge that I'll probably get the same reception from my bio teacher if I don't haul tail to the science wing ASAP, I can't move. But Mr. Freaky Tumor isn't talking. He just looks away, out the window, into the empty quad.

The door swings open. The two of us are still, as if we're posing for a great work of art. Nobody walks into the room at first, but I can sense someone fidgeting in the doorway. Then a soft voice says, "Is everything, like, okay?"

I turn and see a familiar, timid creature, clutching her books against her chest. I think it's the freshman that got me my fries at the game yesterday. Casey. No, Katie. I want to say, "Sure, everything's fine," and flash a big smile, but I can't will my mouth to do either of the above. It just hangs there, so stroke victim–esque.

"Geez, Morgan, you're red! I can get you some water!" she peeps, dropping her books on the table and scurrying out the door.

I walk so that I'm standing above Cam, so close I can rest my chin on the top of his head. I put my hands on his shoulders and force him to look up at me.

"Her who?" I repeat, louder and slower this time.

"Shh, she can hear."

"Cam, we're alone."

"You saw Pip, right? Did he have something with him?"

Though I have no idea what that greasy fellow would have to do with anything, I feel the need to just play along with my nutjob boyfriend, if only to keep him from running down Main

Street naked with a colander on his head later in life. "Um, yeah. He had a pencil box. And his lunch. Well, I think it was his lunch, but he seemed a little whacked about it."

He's silent.

"But what about that guy *isn't* whacked?" I add, tittering nervously, and immediately want to kick myself. I never titter! Why can't he just crack one of his stupid jokes and put me at ease? As I quietly curse this new, more intense version of Cam that is reducing me to behaving like a four-year-old girl, I notice something. There's a brand-new expression dawning on his face. It's . . . fear. "Um, it isn't his lunch, is it?"

"Not even close. Does he have it with him?"

Oh, God, it *is* a severed head. "Um, no. We put it in his locker."

"You *what?*" He looks at the clock, grabs my hand, and pulls me up. "Go to your class. All hell is about to break loose, and I don't want you to be in the middle of it."

"What? No. What's going on?" He's pushing me toward the door, but I resist, trying to dig the heels of my Sam & Libbys into the linoleum.

Just then, Katie rounds the corner, out of breath, a Dixie cup in each hand. She stops short, and before I can react, my chest is covered in something wet. Katie stands there, mouth open like a goldfish. It takes me a moment to realize that (a) it's ice-cold and (b) it's not water; it's some hot-pink stuff that looks sort of like watered-down Pepto. It's like Barbie threw up all over my white cashmere sweater. Blast. "What is that . . . ?" I ask amid the endless apology that's flowing, like a volcanic eruption, from her mouth.

"Hi-C. You looked like you could use something, um, stronger," she squeaks, and then straight back to the regularly scheduled "I'msorryI'msorryI'msorry."

She produces a balled-up Kleenex from her backpack, and as I'm dabbing away at my sweater, I say, "Cam, just let me help—"

But that's when I realize that Cam is gone. Standing where he once was is a painting on an easel—an arrangement of daisies, or a bunch of eggs sunny-side up. Or maybe a portrait? If only that were the most confusing thing on my mind.

So rather than get my second tardy of my school career on the same day as my first, I report to bio as scheduled. Then, I quickly fake a case of massively full bladder and ask Ms. Simpson if I can use the lav pass.

I pace back and forth at Pip's locker, not because I have any clue what is going on, but because I figure that, based on our completely cryptic conversation, if Cam was going to be anywhere, it would be here.

But he's not.

Blast.

All hell's going to break loose. What did he mean by that? He obviously seemed concerned about the thing in Pip's locker. So what can it be? A weapon? Drugs? I haven't yet ruled out the human head, either.

Gah. I don't care if it is a human head. I need to know.

I close my eyes and mouth the word "Fluffernutter" a couple of times, but the beating of my heart drowns out the sound. "Show me Pip," I say.

But nothing comes. A minute passes.

I open my eyes and realize I'm clutching the wooden lav pass so tightly in my hands that splinters are starting to prick my palms.

This isn't working.

Fine. I take a quick look down the hall and, seeing no one, fix my hand on the dial. The first number was twenty-eight, I think. And . . . twelve? I need to start taking ginkgo biloba.

But that's when I hear it.

It starts like a scratching, like the sound of a cat sharpening its claws. At first I think it must be coming from the room behind the row of lockers. Then, the rub-rub-rubbing noise intensifies, to a tinny banging.

Something is inside. Something alive.

That's impossible, I tell myself. Still, my hand is frozen on the lock. Something tells me that Cam is right, that all hell might be breaking loose . . . out of this locker?

And, if so, I'm going to be in the middle of it.

I drop my hand to my side and back away, and as I'm turning to run, I hear it.

A voice, a whisper. But not a sweet-nothings whisper; more of a subhuman hiss.

"Let . . . me . . . out. . . ."

11

As I'm racing down the hall, thinking how nice it would be to be safely ensconced in Ms. Simpson's class, learning about the mollusk phylum, I turn a corner and careen headfirst into Pip and Cam, who, judging from the fact that Pip's breathing like a woman in labor, must have been running toward me.

Cam grabs me by the shoulders. "What's wrong? Why are you screaming?"

I clamp my mouth closed. I was?

"Tell me you didn't go into his locker," he says, breathing hard.

"Um . . ."

"Go back to your class!" he shouts, already several classrooms away, with Pip on his heels like a puppy.

"No!" I tell him, following.

He starts running backward, something all football players seem to be good at, giving me the "Don't make me come over there!" look. Not sure why; he knows that never works with me. Next to him, Pip trips on an invisible bump, falls to the ground like a wounded turkey, then jumps up and keeps running, in this cartoonlike way that somehow allows the heels of his Keds to nearly smack his backside with each and every stride.

Catching up to Pip is easy, but I have to bust a gut to get to Cam. "You have to tell me what is going on. You're going to Pip's locker, right?"

"Yeah."

"There's something alive in there?"

"Damn. You heard her?"

"Her," I repeat mindlessly. "Her? Who . . . ?"

Cam ignores me and turns to Pip. "She's awake. She'll be mad, right?"

All the blood in Pip's body has rushed to his cheeks. "Yes, most definitely."

"How could you leave her in there?"

"I'm sorry. I didn't know what else to do, and I didn't want to arouse suspicions," he explains, clearly upset. As if showing up to school in too-tight cords that amplify your private parts doesn't already have half the school suspicious?

"Her who?" I say, in a whisper. Though I am by no means Godzilla, and in fact think I am quite petite, I can barely squeeze a fist into the lockers they give us. So this "her" must be some sort of tiny animal. Like a girl hamster. Maybe I was hearing things when I heard actual words coming from the locker. I didn't get much sleep last night, after all. Yes, definitely. Pip, fledgling Jeffrey Dahmer that he is, probably just picked up a squirrel on the way to school.

Halfway down the hall, the boys stop short, and I nearly run smack into the wall that is Cam's back, not to mention the freaky tumor. Sliding to a Tom Cruise–style stop on the waxed floor, I begin to itch. My cashmere sweater is clinging to my ribs with perspiration and Katie's sticky pink drink, and it's worse than a thousand mosquito bites. "This sweater is ruined," I grumble, looking down at its pathetic remains.

"Morg–" Cam says.

I step out of his shadow and peer down the hallway. The hall is completely empty, except . . . though we're still several classrooms away, I can see the locker door, number 1687, swinging in the distance. It makes an eerie, tinny screech as it slowly moves back and forth.

Whatever it is, it's out.

"Is anyone concerned about rabies?" I ask.

Cam ignores me. He stares down the hall, eyes fierce. Finally, he says, "I'm sorry. She didn't know."

"Deer ticks are–" Wait. Why isn't he looking at me? I walk around and face him. "Who didn't know?"

"It won't happen again," he murmurs.

"What?" He's not paying attention. It's like he's listening in on another conversation. And his eyes aren't focused down the hallway . . . they're sort of focused on this imaginary spot–this nothingness–right under his nose. He's talking to an imaginary friend.

He really is going nuts.

Helpless, I turn to Pip. "What is he doing?"

"Talking to Dawn," he says softly.

{54}

Dawn? So, perfect, he has an imaginary *girlfriend*. I'm appalled and jealous at once. Is this some psychological disorder that stems from not getting everything one wants out of one's current relationship? "And Dawn is . . . ?" I ask, staring at Cam as he rubs his chin and nods, with deep understanding, at absolutely nothing.

". . . not very happy that we put her in that closed compartment," Pip says.

"So, wait—you can see her, too?" This really wouldn't surprise me.

"No, humans can't see them when they choose not to be seen," he explains.

"Humans?" The word numbs my lips as it passes through them. Because what is Dawn, if she isn't human? And if humans can't see her, but Cam obviously can, what does that make him?

I follow Cam's eyes into the air, concentrating hard on the spot above him, hoping to get a glimpse of whatever he's talking to so that I can confirm that my boyfriend isn't destined for a straitjacket. Finally, when I'm about to give up, I see something move. It's translucent, the color of bubble gum, sort of like a glob of hair gel. A glob of hair gel with a mind of its own, because it's moving in gentle circles and is suspended right above Cam's head.

I blink twice. "What the hell *is* that?" When nobody answers, I look at Pip. "What is that?"

Pip's eyes widen. "Tell her I'm sorry. I didn't know what else to do."

Great. He's ignoring me, too.

I have no idea how anyone can classify gooey hair fixative as either male or female, but I can't concentrate on that right now.

I'm getting more ticked by the minute that Cam finds the blob more worthy of his attention than his own girlfriend.

"Cam," I say softly. He is still going on, very solemnly, to the nothing, about how he'd really prefer things to be kept under wraps right now. It's almost as if *I* don't exist. *"Cam!"*

Startled, he turns toward me. As he does, the pink glob begins to separate and in an instant moves around his head, toward me, in a thousand brilliant and beautiful sparkles. It spreads over me, warm and tingling on my skin, and I can't seem to remember what it was I was going to say. That's when Cam starts to lunge toward me, this wild look in his eyes. A shot of fear runs through my nerves when he reaches for me, yelling, "No, don't!" his mouth frozen in an exaggerated O. Before he can lay a finger on me, though, there's a sudden, blinding pain on the side of my head. The last thing I see is the cold, hard tile stretching up to meet me.

12

"MORGAN?" CAM'S VOICE lures me back.

I open my eyes, but everything is fuzzy shadows, like clouds, like the way I expect heaven would be.

I'm dead.

It's cold in heaven. I'm lying down, under a blanket that feels like burlap, and it smells like perspiration, grass, and lawn fertilizer.

Do people sweat in heaven? And I thought things were just naturally green up there, without the need for harsh chemicals.

Finally, my vision improves to the point where I can make out an old scoreboard, lying on its side, with the faded slogan GO H WKS! I'm on the floor of a cramped storeroom, with cleaning supplies and grass seed on shelves all around, staring down at me.

And the reason the blanket on top of me feels like burlap is because it is. I'm lying down on a gym mat that looks like it was attacked by a team of wildcats, for all the tears in it. The only light in the place is slashing through an air vent near the ceiling, so I can barely make out Cam's face, his lips spread in a straight line.

"Where are we?"

"The shed by the football field."

"Gorgeous. Are you going to explain things to me now?"

"That's why I brought you here," he says.

"Oh, I thought you were just going to ravage my body." I sigh. "Okay. I'm listening. If it isn't a tumor, what is it?"

He's kneeling down next to me, chewing on the underside of his thumb. He never bites his nails; instead, he prefers to go right to his calluses, and he has plenty from all the weight lifting he's done since freshman year. It's the one habit of his I hate, but right now, I don't feel like nagging. And I want to hear the story.

If he will just tell it. Instead, he's inspecting an old pair of gardening gloves nailed to the wall across from us. He appears to have forgotten me. Again.

I snap my fingers. "Hello?"

"Sorry."

"Dawn again?"

"No, I'm just trying to figure out the best way to tell you this."

"Just tell me," I say. We've always been able to tell each other everything, so I'm getting more worried by the second. What could possibly be so bad? He's still looking baffled, so I say, "Here, I'll help. Who the hell hit me?"

"Dawn."

"Dawn? Your imaginary girlfriend?"

He clicks his tongue. "If she hit you, she can't be imaginary, can she?"

"Okay, Mr. Attitude. So she's the pink glob?"

He squints at me. "She's invisible to humans when she wants to be."

I laugh bitterly. "Well, she should work on that trick, because she looks like hair gel to me."

He looks surprised. "You mean, you can see her?"

"I can see *something*. I'm sure I'm just hallucinating or dreaming or insane." I rub the spot on my head.

"I'm sorry about that," he says, dusting some dirt off the knees of his jeans. "She was sleeping when we left for school. We couldn't wake her and knew she would be upset if we left her, so he put her in a paper bag until she woke up."

"Well, that explains her—whoever she is—being pissed. I would be, too, if you treated me like a ham sandwich." I sigh and hold out my hands in exasperation. "This isn't getting much clearer."

"I know. Here. This will explain things." He reaches across the room and pulls out his backpack. He unzips the front pocket and retrieves a crumpled paper bag.

Another paper bag. Great. I peer over as he unfolds it, somehow expecting it to contain all the answers to all the questions that have been swirling in my mind. Finally, he reaches in and pulls out . . .

A stick.

Not like a twig or anything. More like a chopstick. Not even a good set. Just one.

"Is there a fortune cookie, too?" I ask, raising an eyebrow.

"Stop."

I shrug. "I know I shouldn't be making light of the situation, because you're obviously in some emotional turmoil right now, but if you won't let me in on it, what do you expect?"

"Okay, okay. You said a fortune cookie?" Under his breath, half to himself, he says, "I think I could do that."

Staring hard, he holds the stick firmly in his hand, like a pencil, and taps it slowly on the mat beside me, three times.

"It works better with kung pao—" I begin, but before I can get the sentence out, it appears. I blink, then blink again, and finally look at Cam, who is inspecting it thoughtfully.

"See that?" he says.

"See? Yes. Believe?" I murmur.

"Open it. Read it," he urges.

I do as I am told. I pick it up, and it's still warm, but yes, it is a fortune cookie. Just a normal, everyday fortune cookie. One that, I'm sure, didn't exist fifteen seconds ago. Shaking my head, I break it open, pull out the sliver of paper, and read: DON'T LET THEM TAKE ME AWAY FROM YOU.

My eyes trail off the paper, back to his face. The funny thing about Cam is that he'd still like me to think he doesn't cry, even though growing up, I've seen plenty of his meltdowns, from dirty-diaper chaos to the lost-Oreo debacle. And in the split second before I meet his gaze, I know he wipes a tear from the corner of his eye.

13

"WAIT. WHO'S TAKING you away? You're moving? Your dad got relocated? Oh, God!" I bury my face in the disgustingly scratchy burlap.

"No."

"Oh. Then what the hell?" I'm getting frustrated. Nothing's much clearer except for the fact that my amazingly talented boyfriend has the new skill of pulling Chinese food out of his butt. And now he's looking around again, as if trying to zero in on a fly that's been buzzing around his head. "Wait. Are we talking about Dawn again?"

"Shh, she can hear."

Agh. Fine, I'll play along. "Is she here now? Would she like some of this fortune cookie?"

"I don't know. I can't tell."

"Well then, I'm eating it all," I say, shoving a piece into my mouth. Even if it did just come from his butt, I'm starving.

He ignores me, shakes the chopstick in his hand. "I'm not very good with this thing yet."

"'This thing'?"

"My wand."

"Wand? Cam, it's a freaking chopstick."

"A chopstick that can make fortune cookies? Morg, think about it."

I inspect it, then say, dumbly, "But wands are pretty, and gold. With a star at the tip." At least, the one I got at Disney World when I was five was.

"It's a training wand."

Okay, right. So now he is just getting annoying. "Why do you have a wand? Are you a magician? Is Dawn your assistant? And you made her invisible?"

"No, she's my guide."

"Your . . . guide? Like a tour guide? For wherever you're being taken?"

"Right."

"Okay. So where are you being taken?"

"I'm not sure. To wherever it is that fairies go."

"You mean, like, Middle Earth or something?" I look down and see the broken remains of the fortune cookie, and I can't keep the sarcasm from creeping back into my voice. "So, um. Some fairies want to kidnap you. Why? Do you have the one ring to rule them all?"

"They've come to take me home," he says softly.

"Oh." This would be the time that I'd expect a camera crew to come bursting through the door, saying this is all a practical joke. But Cam doesn't joke like that. He's a terrible liar. I study the door, willing for it to open, for some peppy TV host to thrust a mike under my nose and ask me how it feels to know I fell for the stupidest and most unbelievable prank ever, but it never happens.

"Wait. Are you saying you're a fairy? Like Tinker Bell?"

"Well, not exactly. Tinker Bell was a pixie, and she isn't real."

I'm suddenly aware that my mouth is hanging open. I close it and firmly place my hand on his shoulder. "Listen to yourself. That's nuts. You got hit too hard last night, and—"

"I know it sounds crazy, but what about the fortune cookie?"

"Big deal." I point to the pimple budding from my chin. "Make this go away, and maybe I'll believe you."

"I can't. I told you, I'm not so good with the wand yet. I wouldn't want to turn you into anything."

I roll my eyes. "Fantastic. So, where are they taking you?"

Since Cam has never wigged out on me like this before, I keep my lips zipped as to where I think he needs to go: the nearest mental institution. "It's this kingdom, this whole other world," he says, his voice wavering. "I'm not sure. Dawn told me it exists alongside this world. I know, it's totally whacked, but I have to go there on my sixteenth birthday—"

"What do you mean by 'have to'?" My voice starts to do the same little dance that his is doing, rising and falling between a whisper and a nervous shriek. "Because we have this party, and everyone's going to be there, and . . . "

He's staring at me, and I know exactly what he's thinking: *I just found out I'm not human, and you're worried about your sweet sixteen?*

And yes, it may be a little callous of me, but please. A fairy? I know everything about this boy. He's always been completely levelheaded, never one to believe the latest gossip, no matter how true it seems. And there isn't anything about him that is a mystery to me. I know when he's angry, I know when he's nervous, I know when he's . . . lying.

And, looking at him now, I can tell one thing for certain.

He believes every word he is saying.

"This is crazy," I say, my voice hoarse. "You're telling me that a week from now, a bunch of fairies are going to steal you from me?"

He nods.

"For how long?"

He doesn't answer, just looks away. I take that as a "forever."

I bite my tongue. "This has got to be a dream. Wake up, Morgan," I mumble, pinching my arm through my cashmere sweater.

He ignores me, stands up, opens the door a crack, and peers out. "Look, we haven't got much time. Are you going to help me or not?"

My head is still throbbing, but I sit up and pull my knees under me. "What do you want me to do?"

He relaxes a little. "Do you remember how we learned, a few years back in world history, about those women in China? How the men liked small feet, so the women used to bind them?"

"Uh-huh," I say, flashing back to an image of a poor Chinese woman with feet that were no bigger than balled-up fists. They'd actually been able to stunt the growth of their feet by wrapping them tightly. Gross. "So what?"

"I figure it's worth a shot." He reaches into his bag again, and this time he produces a roll of white bandage. He looks around carefully, then, pulling up his T-shirt, whispers, "Will you wrap my wings?"

{64}

14

THE REST OF the day is a bit of a haze to me. I end up missing bio and most of lunch because of Cam. When I finish wrapping up Cam's wings—yes, you heard me right, *wings*—I skulk out of the shed, knowing something big, something life-altering, is happening but not being fully able to comprehend what that something is. I find myself so deep in confusion that I'm barely able to walk a straight line.

My boyfriend is a fairy. Cam has always been talented, almost superhuman, so I'd fully expected him to do something fantastic, like one day end up on the cover of *SI,* but flying around, painting rainbows, taking teeth away from under children's pillows in the night? I saw the wings, the fortune cookie that materialized out of nowhere, and yet . . . I've known this boy since we were in diapers. I know him and his family inside and out. It isn't as if he suddenly appeared in a flower bed one day after a thunderstorm, or as if his parents are mysterious elvish royalty. And he burps and farts like any good human—in fact, quite a bit more than I'd like.

As I was wrapping the bandage around his shoulder blades, trying my best not to come into any contact with the growth, he told me that the wings are actually just for show; that, according to Dawn, he can fly. Which explains his Superman on the football field. Dawn had told him to be very careful, because the reason he blacked out last night is because his powers are not fully developed. He is just a newbie now, but on his sixteenth birthday, when he fully inherits his powers, he will have to leave this world.

Forever.

But if he is a fairy, and if he does have to leave, that would explain why I hardly ever see him in any visions of the future. His best friend, Scab, is my biggest fan and best customer. I've seen almost all of his next five years: the game where he dislocates his shoulder, the graduation party where he eats sixty hot wings in twelve minutes, his college years in Miami. One would expect Cam to be somewhere in the background, but he never is. I hadn't realized it until today, but I haven't seen him in any visions further out than two weeks from now. As for my own future, I've tried to imagine it only a handful of times, and it's always been too fuzzy to comprehend. It's a close-up of my nostril, or a big shot of my butt, and the "camera," which obviously has a sense of humor, never pans out. Still, I've always felt like Cam is somewhere nearby. He just *has* to be.

But maybe he isn't.

Oh, God.

After that realization, I end up spending much of my time in the third stall of the music-wing bathroom, having a minor mental breakdown and vowing never to wear my orange-sherbet-colored flip-flops again. If it weren't for them, Sierra Martin wouldn't have recognized my feet and begun peppering me with questions about her future while I was trying to stem the tide of tears that were majorly schlubbing up my complexion.

"*No comprendo,*" I say in the best accent my two years of Spanish will allow. "*Soy una . . .*" How the hell do you say "ESL student"? "Um. *Soy una biblioteca mas grande.*"

Close enough.

"Hello, Morgan? Are you there?" she asks, after a moment of silence. I think the flu is easier to avoid.

"No! No Morgan. *No comprendo. Baja en el ascensor,*" I say combatively.

"Morgan, stop," she whines. "You're totally freaking me out. I just need to ask you a teensy-weensy favor."

"Fine." I give in. I flush a tear-soaked wad of TP and open the door, hoping that my face doesn't look as red and blotchy as a volcanic eruption. If it does, she doesn't seem to notice. Of course, I think she may be oblivious to anything other than her stupid future. "Great timing."

She examines her hair in the mirror and fluffs this giant, fluorescent-pink feather thing that's holding up her ponytail. "Well, what do you expect? I've been in *agony*. And you didn't return my calls."

"Calls?" I ask innocently, even though I programmed my phone to play "Super Freak" whenever her number pops up so that I can let it go right into voice mail. Which happened, in the past twenty-four hours, around fifty times.

"Yeah. This is important stuff."

"I know. I've just been . . ." I take a look in the mirror and gasp. I've just been auditioning for *The New Addams Family*? I think the school administration purposely installs fluorescent lighting that would make Heidi Klum look like the undead because they want to smoke us out of there as soon as possible. But I look more undead than usual, and I am not exaggerating. In the less than two hours since getting whopped on the head by that demented mosquito, I've transformed into something Frankensteiny. I rub a smudge of black eyeliner that has some-how migrated to my lower cheek away. "Busy."

"Well. You know your 'vision'?" She says this with a roll of the eyes.

I nod, grabbing on to the corners of the sink for support. Here it comes.

"Well, I most definitely think you were thinking of the wrong person."

"I know. You told me that."

She holds up her finger. "I brought supporting evidence. If I am going to ever be an attorney with one of the top firms in New York, I should be able to argue this. Exhibit A." She reaches into her stack of books and pulls out a stub of paper. "Do you know what this is?"

God, no.

"It's a ticket from my trip to the Metuchen Fair. I went there this weekend. And I stopped by Madame Babuska's tent. And guess what she said?"

I sigh. At least Madame Babuska is smart enough to charge twenty bucks for her fortunes. "That you're going to Harvard?"

"Yes!" She shrugs. "Well, no. She said that I am going to find the love of my life next year and his name is Harvey. I figure that's pretty close."

"Pretty . . . ," I say. How can I think about this when my boyfriend is growing wings as we speak?

"But that's not all. Exhibit B." She waves her hands in front of her. "I totally wouldn't even go to MCC if my life depended on it. Like, if every other college in the world turned me down, I would just kill myself. See? It's virtually impossible for you to have envisioned that."

"What if your suicide attempt failed and left you brain damaged?" I ask. "It could happen. I saw it once on *Oprah*."

Oprah. Cam and I used to watch it together when he wasn't at practice. I would cry during all the inspirational stories, and he would make fun of me. Ah, the good old days. Sierra starts to pull out Exhibit C just as another tear starts to force its way out.

I stop her. "Yeah. You're right. I guess I was wrong."

She smiles. "Really?"

No, not really, but I can't take it anymore. At this point, my mind is focused on only one thing. Well, three things. Cam. And his wings.

Anyway, something in my life goes right. Sierra gives me an excited hug and prances out of the room, triumphant.

I miraculously manage to make it home without getting hit by a school bus. When I get there, though, I don't feel like going inside. Instead, I get this weird idea to lie on the grass and stare up at the sky. Maybe because this is something Cam and I used to do a lot when we were growing up, and I've been thinking about our past a lot today, trying to recollect if there had been signs of him not being of this world prior to last night. No, he had always been so normal. I can remember shouting out,

"Look! I see an angel!" and Cam, always practical, would say, "That's just a cumulus. There's a front moving in." I'd always thought he'd grow up to be a weatherman.

Well, today certainly threw a wrench into those plans. Fairies don't predict the weather. I think they make the weather. Or something.

I crawl into the grass, catlike, then flop over and stare. There are more clouds than peeks of blue sky, though I could really, really use that blue sky right now.

I hear the engine of a car, then look past my feet, to see my father's minivan rounding the corner into our driveway. A door slams and his voice calls, "What could be so bad that it's worth missing *General Hospital* for?"

My father loves the soaps. He watches *General Hospital* religiously and has molded his work schedule at the hospital so that he goes in at four in the morning and comes home right in time to watch his shows. Every Sunday, he reads *Soap Opera Digest* and inevitably will give me the latest update on his "retirement countdown," when he will finally be home to watch them all. What a glorious (for him) and altogether mortifying (for me) day it will be when my dad can sit at home in his boxers all day, watching the soaps. I am certain the garbage in the house would never get taken out if he knew that TiVo exists.

"Daddy," I complain, twisting a blade of grass between my fingers, "Ms. Simpson is probably going to call you about me missing bio. And Cam's a fairy. What do I do?"

I hear the screen door open and close. "It's on! It's on!" he shouts from inside.

I groan and close my eyes. "I'll be in, in a minute."

I hear the swish of grass as someone collapses next to me like a wounded cow. My suspicions are confirmed when I lift my head an inch from the ground and see the scuffed Keds, toes pointing to the sky in a V. Not exactly someone I want to talk to right now, but, for some reason, I can't move.

"What is the purpose of reclining here?" he asks me gently.

"Because I can't breathe. I think I'm going to die." I sit up, pull my knees to my chest, and look down at my ruined cashmere sweater, spattered with sticky pink stains. "Are you a fairy, too? Is that why you appeared out of nowhere?"

He shakes his head. "I am the Brownes' son."

"You mean, you're Cam's brother?"

"No." He looks at the sky as if searching for the right words. "Fairies like to play tricks on humans. They're jealous. They like to steal human babies. On the night I was born, the hospital must have left a window open, because the fairies took me and left Cam."

"Why? Why would they leave him?"

"Cam was a changeling. A sickly fairy. He was supposed to die of illness before he reached adulthood."

"But he's not sick. Well, not anymore. He used to have bad asthma when he was younger, but he's fine now."

"They do not understand why he recuperated. And they need him, as there has been a terrible tragedy. So they've come to take him back."

"Tragedy?"

"Yes, Cameron's older brother, Azizl, has been killed, and now his father has no true heir."

"So they want to trade you for an heir?"

He nods.

I exhale deeply. "Well, why are they still here, then? Why

didn't they just take him and get the hell out, like they did the day he was born?"

"There is a portal between the two worlds," Pip explains. "Fairies—or anyone, for that matter—may always pass into this world. But the portal to the fairy world is open only at midnight on Day of Birth and Day of Becoming."

"Day of who?"

"Becoming. Their sixteenth birthday."

Blades of wet, green grass prick at my legs, but I can't feel a thing because I'm numb. "So you're the Brownes' consolation prize for losing Cam? That's—inhuman." I pause, realizing that, duh, it's probably inhuman because they're not human. "I mean, it must feel horrible."

"It did come as a shock to Mr. and Mrs. Browne."

"Well, obviously. But I'm talking about you. It must feel horrible for you."

"I do miss the beauty of the fairy world, and this place is very different, and ugly, to me," he concedes. "But they don't want me there anymore. They want Cameron."

"That's a terrible thing to do. To steal you from your parents, then throw you away? Aren't you pissed?"

His eyes narrow. "Pissed?"

"Angry. Upset. They threw Cam away when they thought he was no good, and now they're throwing you away." I collapse back onto the grass and stare up at the clouds again, when I realize I'm more rattled by it than he is. "Don't you care?"

He shrugs. "I wasn't upset when they cast me out because I never really felt like I belonged there. I guess I was hoping that I would fit in better here. But . . ."

From the pathetic look on his face, I know what he is going

to say, and I know that he's right. "But you don't fit in here, either."

He nods. "Everybody looks at me just like they did there. I thought it would be different here because I'm one of your kind. But it's not, and now I wonder if it was a mistake, my coming here. At least I understood how things worked in Otherworld."

Otherworld. So that is the name of the world responsible for taking Cam away from me. The source of my wrath. Stupid world.

When the first raindrop smacks me right between the eyes, the answer hits me. "Can't I reason with them?"

"Pardon?" he asks politely, very much like an old Southern lady.

"They want Cam because they think he's more like them, right?"

"Right."

"Well, it's obvious that they're wrong. I just need to explain things."

"Er, Cameron is more like them. He *is* a fairy."

"So? There are other things to being a fairy, I'm sure, than just having wings. I mean, Cam doesn't fit the fairy mold at all. If I saw the two of you together, I would instantly think *you* were the fairy. You have that dainty fairy air going for you. And you know the fairy ways. You said yourself that you think it was a mistake, coming here, and that you *want* to go back. Cam doesn't."

"I don't think it is possible for me to go back there," he says, weaving his long fingers together so tightly that his knobby knuckles turn white. "Cam is the only true heir, and they want him. They want me here. And it isn't wise to tell a fairy she's wrong."

Whatever. Pip seems so weak and mild-mannered that he wouldn't think it was wise to tell his own grandmother she was wrong. "Who do I need to talk to? That Dawn chick?"

He closes his lips tightly. There are goose bumps on his pencil-like arms, and his legs are trembling in his too-tight trousers. "Yes, she is Cameron's intended."

"Intended?" My heart protests, beating hard against the wall of my chest. "Intended" as in "intended to be together forever"? Like we once were? Nooo . . . that is so totally wrong, on so many levels. "What does that mean? I thought she was his guide."

"For now, but when he is back in Otherworld, they will be married."

"Married?" Now I really can't breathe. No, no, no, this cannot be happening. There is no way my boyfriend is going to marry that half-invisible skank. I collect myself and say, "We'll just have to see about that. Where can I find her?"

I hadn't noticed that the rain had picked up, and as I struggle to my feet, long whips of wet hair slap my face. It occurs to me that the reason Dawn whopped me upside the head is because she's jealous, because she realizes there's no way Cam would be with her, a gnat, when he could have a real woman like me. And I'm used to dealing with pathetic, jealous girls. I do it every day. So what if this one has wings?

He's up on his elbows. "What are you going to do?"

"Nothing. Just bitch-slap her back to whatever other world she came from. Cam is mine."

He flails about on the grass like a one-winged moth, then finally staggers to his feet. His once-slicked-back hair, dark with rain, is hanging in his eyes, and as he blinks the water from them, for a second he reminds me of Cam on the sidelines during a downpour. "I . . . don't know if . . . you should . . ."

"Spit it out. Where is she?"

I'm so busy sharpening my sword, thinking of just the right words, that I don't realize his cheeks have turned the color of the storm clouds.

"Right behind you."

15

THE FEAR STARTS in my stomach. As the tingles radiate to my fingers and toes, I decide that maybe bitch-slapping her back to whatever other world would possibly—no, definitely—be taken as an insult. I'm in trouble.

I turn around, thinking how warped my life has become to have sunk to the level of apologizing to a glob of hair fixative. Instead, I come nearly nose to nose with a perfect, glowingly clear complexion that even all the Proactiv-pushing celebs would kill for. Giant, almond-shaped blue eyes, surrounded almost fully by an aura of lush platinum hair, the stuff of Pantene commercials. Her cotton-candy lips are slightly parted, leaking no emotion whatsoever, but I can already tell they're the kind that always speak sex, no matter what she's saying.

This is my boyfriend's "intended."

I feel the overwhelming need to drown my head in the nearest toilet.

When she opens her mouth to speak, I brace myself for war. But she says, "You wanted to see me?" just as innocently as a child.

I take a step back and inspect her, hoping for an ass the size of a Buick or something. Unfortunately, there's nothing to detract from the perfect-ten thing she has going on. She's impossibly skinny, probably into negative sizes. I pause on her jeans—yes, real Seven jeans. Not a dress spun from spiderwebs or corn silk or whatever I'd been expecting. And no pointy shoes with little bells on them; she's wearing high boots with three-inch heels. She looks completely out of place on my front lawn, like she should be parading down a runway or shaking her ass on a dance floor with Paris Hilton.

"You're Dawn?" I ask doubtfully. "Where are your wings?"

"Shape-shifting is easy for we of the Seelie Court, the most powerful fairies in all of Otherworld," she explains, a little too snootily for my taste.

Ah, shape-shifting. Of course. Nobody can look that good naturally. Out of all the human forms she could take on, common sense would dictate choosing a shape like one of America's Next Top Models. I'm certain that as far as fairies go, she probably looks like a megatroll.

"Seelie Court?" I put my hands on my hips to show I'm not swayed by her "power."

Pip whispers into my ear, "The Seelie Court are the most benevolent fairies. They are kind and good to humans."

I whirl around to him. "Oh, yeah, really kind. Let's not forget, she *hit* me."

He shrugs. "Um. Usually."

I think for a moment. "So, you're, like, a fairy godmother?"

She nods, pleased with herself.

"Let me get this straight. *You* are a fairy godmother?" I ask, wondering if the whole motherly-and-chubby thing was only something Disney invented.

"Silence, Dubbleflinger," she says to me, then looks at Pip. Dismissing me, just like that. Wench.

I look at Pip, who is fidgeting. I don't think he has made eye contact once with Dawn. "What is a Dubbleflinger?"

He looks at the ground. "I–I am not quite sure."

"Liar," I hiss at him. I know it's something bad. And if she thinks she can hurl insults at me, she'd better be prepared for the bitch-slapping of her young life.

She says to Pip, "The training has been going well, but slowly, due to"–she glares at me–"*some* interruptions. I am sure he's just in shock. This is unusual news, I suppose. But I know he'll eventually come around."

"Hey, look." I snap my fingers in her face. "He's not coming around. He doesn't want to be a fairy."

She rolls her eyes. "Of course he does. He just doesn't know enough about it yet, so he's afraid. It is his birthright to join the Seelie Court."

"What? No, you see, he's in love with me."

She laughs as if I'm a child who just said something amusing but completely misguided. "That is ridiculous. Fairies are not capable of that. And he is more important than you can possibly comprehend. He shall be our king."

"King?" I spit out. "You mean, as in . . ." I try to find something similar, but my mind is completely blank. ". . . king?"

What does she know? Cam is very generous in sharing the last Chips Ahoy! in the tray and always buys me popcorn when we go to the movies, but he doesn't exactly fit the fairy godmother mold. And, while the idea of his being king is well and good, Cam can't rule a whole kingdom, since he can barely keep his own closet from smelling like feet. "No, believe me, he doesn't want to. He will never want to. So you can just pack up your bibbity-bobbity bags and get the hell . . ."

My voice trails off when I realize I'm, again, creeping up there on the harsh-o-meter. That's probably not a great idea, considering she's Miss All-Powerful and everything.

She smiles at me, almost warmly, and leans in. Her voice is even, and sweet: "Cameron is coming home with me on his sixteenth birthday. If you interfere, what I did to you this morning will feel like a gentle breeze, compared with what I will do."

I take a step back and look at Pip. He may have just peed his pants. And maybe he has good reason—if the fairy godmother in *Cinderella* could turn mice into horses and an ordinary pumpkin into a pretty pimped-up ride, what could this one do to me?

Something tells me that life as a horse would probably not be all that wonderful.

Kind and benevolent, my butt.

She's staring at me expectantly, finger on the trigger, ready to cast that spell over me should I say the wrong thing. Though my heart is crying other things, my head says, *Shut up, Morgan.* I am acutely aware now that the rain has soaked me completely, and as the chill overtakes my body, one fact is obvious.

I am going to lose my boyfriend. Forever.

16

BEN & JERRY'S S'mores ice cream is low-fat, but it defeats the purpose when you swallow an entire pint in one mouthful. But so what? My perfect boyfriend is a fairy, due to marry next month's *Cosmo* cover, leaving me here with a face full of worry zits and an ever-expanding waistline. Even if I were interested in finding a replacement, there are no other guys at Stevens that even compare. I might as well cancel my Bally's membership and get a frequent-diner card for Burger King.

I've missed all of *General Hospital,* so my father feels it necessary to give me the blow-by-blow of who's having whose baby and which doctors ended up in bed together. As he's babbling on, my mother, thankfully, interrupts. "Are you sure you don't want any meat loaf?"

Oblivious, I'd scooped the entire carton of B&J into my salad bowl and downed it before her latest culinary masterpiece had even come out of the oven. "Um, sorry. I'm full."

"I bet," she says, frowning at the dish, which is caked in chocolate. She's Italian, so this is blasphemy. She told me once that her mother chased one of her past boyfriends out of the house with a rolling pin for not liking pot cheese. Another got slammed against a wall for not being able to pronounce *cavatelli* correctly. In her family, there is no such thing as "full." And, since my father tips the scales, he fits right in. Cam used to fit in, too; my mother worshipped his appetite like Eden worships his feats on the field. Though he isn't nearly as big as my dad, his regular workouts leave him famished, so my mother would always get a little weak in the knees whenever I'd announce he'd be eating over, which was once or twice a week. I can just remember him smiling devilishly, asking, "Mrs. Sparks, would you mind if I had thirds on those manicotti?" He even pronounced it correctly, *monny GOT.*

But I guess that won't be happening anymore.

My mother's words stop me before I attempt to slash my wrists with the butter knife. "Did you happen to find out who that handsome young man is?" she asks.

"Who?" I rub my eye, then realize she's talking about Pip. That stud. "Oh. Yeah."

There's this long pause, and then my mother says, "Well?"

I figured my mother would have found out by now, with her amazing abilities of perception, which include peeking in neighbors' windows and popping over to drop off some mail that was accidentally delivered to our address (though the fact is that my mother just "accidentally" got our mail out of the wrong mailbox). I don't feel like launching into the whole explanation, so I just say, "He's a cousin, I think."

My mother asks another question, but I'm not listening. From my seat at the table, I can see the window to Cam's room. The light switches on just as my mother says, "Hon, you okay?"

Cam is home from practice.

I jump from my seat. "Fine!" I shout, a little too desperately, then wipe my mouth with my napkin. "May I be excused?"

We need to talk. If he really, truly is going to be leaving me forever on his sixteenth birthday, that gives us only a week. And I have no idea who I'll be then, because I've never had to define myself without him.

17

I'VE ALWAYS THOUGHT Mr. and Mrs. Browne were from another planet, because they're just too perfect. Mrs. Browne is always dressed in some smart, accessorized outfit that could easily put her on the cover of *Good Housekeeping*, and Mr. Browne looks like a graying movie star. Really, it's ironic that *Cam* is the one that isn't from this world.

So I'm shocked when the door swings open and a lifeless Mrs. Browne stands there, looking like she hasn't slept in a week. Her hair is out of control, and her designer clothes hang on her slumped shoulders, making her look twice her age. Usually, she'll greet me with a peppy "Hi, Morgan dear!" but instead, she breaks into tears, heavy sobs that shake her small body. She opens the screen door and pulls me into her arms and hugs me so close I almost throw up the ice cream I've just eaten. It's weird, because I've known her forever, and I think this is the first time she's actually cried in front of me. And hugged me. And made me want to vomit.

"So, I guess you guys know about this," I say when she pulls back.

Her lower lip trembles. She can't bring herself to speak. I exhale with relief. At least someone else knows how I feel.

Finally, she says, "It's terrible, isn't it?"

I nod. "How is Mr. Browne?"

"He wants to sue the hospital. As if anyone would believe that fairies came in the day our son was born and switched him." She sighs. "He's obviously not thinking straight. What we should be thinking about is how to help our sons through this."

"Our sons." It sounds strange, but I knew Mrs. Browne would be so diplomatic. "There has to be a way we can keep Cam here."

She looks away, tears in her eyes. "I don't think there is. But if you think of something, let me know." She gnaws on her bottom lip. "I can't believe Cameron will be gone in only a few days."

She's about to start sobbing again, so I say, "Pip is your real son."

"Yes. He has Mr. Browne's laugh," she adds with a sad smile. "And that's another thing entirely. To know that I couldn't be with him when he was growing up . . . I asked him if they took good care of him in Otherworld, but the poor child didn't want to talk about it."

"Really?" I ask, surprised. I'd had a hard time getting Pip to shut up about the fairies. "I'm sure he doesn't blame you."

She nods absently, then shakes herself back into reality. She almost sounds like the old Mrs. Browne when she says, "I know you're not here to cry with me all night. Cam is upstairs."

I'm climbing the stairs to his room when his door opens a couple of inches. Cam slides out sideways, then carefully closes the door, so that it barely clicks behind him. He's startled when he sees me, but then relaxes. "Hey, you. I was just coming to see you."

"You were?" I'm happy he didn't forget all about me, which I thought might happen with the Blond Bombshell in the way. I point to his room. "What's going on in there?"

He sighs. "Dawn has this fairy tutorial thing going on. She's a pocket-sized Hitler."

I grin. Same old Cam. Of course he didn't forget about me.

"I'm ditching lesson nine. It's all about humans and how to interact with them, and I think I know enough about that."

"Why even do it at all?" I mutter.

"I'm wondering the same thing. I've spent all afternoon on this . . . and for what?"

"All afternoon? What happened to football practice?"

His face turns grim. "I tried. All my passes were falling short. I couldn't complete a single throw. Coach said I needed to take some time off and rest my arm, so he told me to pack it in early. I feel different . . . weak."

"Oh." He slides his arms under mine and pulls me close. I lean in, pull him to me. I can feel the bandages, those damn bandages, and know that from now on, every embrace will remind me of our inevitable parting. And when I bury my face in his chest, I know that's not the only reminder. I pull away quickly. Something is wrong. His normal, natural scent—half-woodsy, like wet grass, half-spicy, like barbershop aftershave—is gone. "You . . . smell different."

He pulls me in again, and I feel his breath on my hair. "I'm not surprised. A lot about me is different."

I gulp. If the fairies have the power to strip him of his yummy, human smell, can they change the way he feels about me, too? "Like what?"

"I can barely bench-press one eighty now. Last week I was up to two twenty-five. But I think I can see better. And hear better. It's . . ." He stops when he sees the expression on my face. "That won't change, Boo."

"Huh?"

He points up to the ceiling, then puts his finger to his mouth in a "shh" gesture.

I look up, a prickling sensation running up my spine. I squint through the minimal light coming from the kitchen, searching for the pink glob, but I can't see anything. "What? You mean she's here?"

He shrugs. "I know what you're thinking."

I blush, wondering if it's that obvious that I'm a total wuss, scared to death of getting my ass kicked again by a fairy.

"Fairies have heightened awareness of everything around them." Then he leans in and whispers, "That will *never* change. Got that?"

Oh, he's talking about us. The way he feels about me. As much of a relief as it is, I can't help wanting to follow it up with a million questions to solidify those feelings. But I can't. Not here. I'm frozen in place, wondering if my next words will unwittingly force me into life as a quadruped. I whisper, "Isn't there a way we can be alone?"

"Yeah." He takes me by the wrist and leads me across the hall, into the bathroom. He shuts the door behind me, turns on the faucet, then cranks up the shower. "Get in."

I stare at him. "Um. I said 'alone,' not 'wet.'"

He matches my stare with a look so commanding, I never would have thought he had it in him. He has always been an easygoing guy, so this "fairy royal" stuff must be doing *mucho* for his leadership skills. I lean over and pull off my ballet flats, then slip behind the curtain, into the water. Pellets of ice sting my shoulders. "Hello! Freezing!"

"Sorry." His hand fumbles in and turns up the metal handle with the *H* on it. I cross my arms over my chest as the water soaks my white shirt through to near transparency. Leaning over to avoid hitting the curtain rod with his forehead, he steps in, his faded jeans immediately splattered with dark indigo. As I'm thinking this has to be a ploy to get me in his own private wet T-shirt contest, he says, "I guess I'm not enough of a fairy yet. If a fairy comes into contact with running water, they can die. So we're safe here."

"I didn't know fairies could die," I say, hiding my excitement over this discovery. "But that's what Pip had said. About your brother?"

"Supposedly he was killed in a war. He was Massif's elder son, and heir to the throne. Until they remembered me. When I turn sixteen, they say I can be king. Can you believe that?" There's disgust in his face. "I can't. This so freaking warped."

"And don't forget the part about Dawn," I say, wrapping my arms around me.

He rolls his eyes and shakes his head. "Don't remind me."

"She's a witch. She threatened me," I blurt out. It feels good to finally feel safe enough to say it.

"She what?"

"I think she might hurt me even worse than before if I interfere."

"No, she won't. She wouldn't do that to me. I had a talk with her. She knows I'd kill her first."

"But you're supposed to get"—and I nearly choke on this next word—"married."

"Marriage there is not like it is here. It's not about love. It's about uniting two powerful kingdoms," he says, to calm me down.

"She said something about fairies not being capable of love. Is that true?"

He shakes his head. "No way. If it is, then I guess I'm not a fairy."

I smile at him, since that was exactly the reaction I'd hoped for. "Okay, so what do we do? Flush Dawn down the toilet?"

"No, Dawn isn't the problem. It's Massif. He is the one who arranged this marriage."

"Is he as reasonable as she is?"

"Dawn is only following his orders. But I told you. If I go with them, it's forever. I won't be able to see you again. And I'm not leaving you."

His T-shirt is getting wet now, matting against his chest, his back. His chest, while once firmly defined, looks less so, but the mound on his back seems larger. He is changing, and there is nothing he can do to stop it. "How are your wings coming along?" I ask softly.

He looks disgustedly over his shoulder. "I don't care if they put me in the Smithsonian Institution and make me the world's first fairy lab rat. I'm not going."

His eyes blaze with intensity, and so I feel the need to lean in and hold him. The water is warmer now, nice when it mixes with our lingering good-night kiss. When we say our "One, two, three," I'm half-dazed.

I slosh back to my bedroom after the rain has stopped. Luckily, my parents are engrossed in an episode of *Law and Order,* so I'm spared the third degree over looking like an extra from *Titanic.* I quickly slip upstairs, thankful to feel the heat of the blow-dryer on me. While I'm standing there, absently running the brush through my hair, I catch a glimpse of something on the nightstand reflected in the mirror. It's the picture of Cam and me on the roller coaster.

Things aren't as bad as they seem.

I shake my head and turn off the dryer. The only thing I know is that they aren't as good as they could be.

Afterward, I look for some boxers and a tank to sleep in, but my mother must not have done this week's laundry, because my dressers are half-empty. I reach into my night-table drawer and find one of Cam's glossy number 10 jerseys, then pull it over my head. The scent of grass and barbershop cologne soothes me. I fall asleep clutching the fabric to my face and letting it mop up my tears.

18

THE FLUORESCENT-ORANGE paper on the bulletin board in the library says, BE SOMEBODY! NATIONAL HONOR SOCIETY APPLICATIONS DUE MONDAY, OCTOBER 11. I'm by no means interested, but I have nothing better to do. Nobody goes to the library on Friday, so I figured I could spend my first-period study hall here, alone, with the hopes that by second period, the swelling in my face will have subsided. A night of crying, coupled with the beating I took from that little gnat, has given me the ugliest, reddest cheeks on the planet. With five minutes left in the period, I catch my reflection in the chrome of the water fountain across the hall and realize it's not going to happen. Even a glob of hair gel is more appealing than I am.

Cam doesn't want to go. That fact in itself should be enough, but because these demented fairies have absolutely no sense, we have to resort to plan B. And, since Dawn is constantly around Cam, surveying his every move, it's up to me. I need to come up with a plan.

But my head feels like it's cracking open. My mind is blank.

As I'm packing up my books, Eden pokes her head in, then smiles big and bounds over to me. She's wearing a T-shirt that says LOVE UNIVERSITY in big, black letters and pink flip-flops that make an obnoxious smacking noise as she hurries through the silent library. She doesn't seem to notice. "What up, girl?"

Eden's efforts to sound like a homegirl always miss the mark, but I can't help but grin. Eden, my port in the storm. My beacon in the cold, dark night. The peanut butter to my jelly. My—

"Wow, you look terrible! What happened to your head?"

"Um, nothing. I—"

"Your face looks blotchy." She looks up at the bulletin board and says, "What? Are you thinking of applying for NHS?"

"No, not really."

"Didn't think you would."

I glare at her. "What do you mean? I could. I have a four-oh."

She shrugs. "You never do any of that stuff. And for NHS, you need to have some extracurricular activities. Remember when cheerleading tryouts were coming up? I told you. It looks good on your college app. But you were busy."

I vaguely remember the conversation. I always space when she brings up cheerleading, since it happens every day, so I probably told her "no way in hell" without batting an eyelash. Yes, cheerleaders go to all the football games, but they have to cheer at the basketball games, too, and what fun would it be if Cam wasn't there? There had been other opportunities—the school paper, the yearbook, the Key Club—but I'd nixed them all. Because none of them could promise as much fun as kicking back, goofing off with Cam. My Cam.

I know it must sound pathetic, but everything about my life is woven to Cam's. Our interests, our circle of friends, our futures . . . everything is intertwined. We are two sides of a coin. And when one side ceases to exist, what happens to the other one?

I throw my books on a table and bury my face in my hands, just as the waterworks start up again.

"Morgan?" I feel Eden's arms around me. I lean into her and let out a muffled sob on her shoulder. "Oh, hon. It's okay. The honor society would be lucky to have you."

Honor society? Who can think of the honor society at a time like this? The bell rings, signaling the end of the period. I straighten and wipe a tear from my eye as nonchalantly as possible and inspect the pad of my finger, hoping to make this recent breakdown appear to be nothing more than a fleck of dust caught in my eye. I cannot go around weeping all day. People will think I've lost it. "I'm fine."

"This isn't about Cam again, is it? About that vision you had?" she asks, shaking her head at me pitifully. "He's been acting different."

"What isn't different about him?" I mutter.

The hallways are packed with kids moving to class, but I spot a lanky form shuffling past the library, almost as if he's cross-country skiing. He's wearing lame old-style green sweatpants so big that the fabric pools over the elastic ankle bands, past his feet. He peers in for a moment but keeps moving, his hands out in front of him, limp, as if playing the piano. I immediately feel bad for him. No, he doesn't fit in. And maybe, with Cam gone, I won't fit in, either. He's lost something dear to him, too, so maybe he would understand the way I feel. Maybe we could be friends.

Eden catches me staring at him and her voice becomes serious. "Did you hear what happened?"

"No, what?" I say offhandedly, checking the disaster that is my face in my pocket mirror. Eden has a way of following the most world-coming-to-an-end warning with, "I spilled raspberry sauce on my Sevens!" or, "There's a new episode of *Lost* on tonight!" Snore.

"With that Pip guy?"

I look up. "What?"

"He was wearing these really funny cords today. You know?"

I nod. I know. God, I wish I didn't, but I know.

"Well, Scab tried to give him a wedgie, but couldn't because they were so tight. And so a bunch of the guys tackled him to the ground and stole his pants."

"They what?" I shake my head. "That's so wrong. The football team did that?"

"Yeah, but you have to agree, the pants needed to go."

Cam had had to stay back home to complete another one of the Evil Gnat's lessons, but if he'd been there, he would have tried to stop them. He'd have done it because Pip is the Brownes' real son, and, well, just because. That's the kind of guy he is—a man among boys. And so it just figures that the fairies want to take him from me, not to mention on the most important night of my teenage life, my sweet sixteen. I already have a lot on my mind, so I don't need to add babysitting Pip to the list, but, well . . . it's what Cam would do.

"Scab had better lay off," I say. To her questioning look, I add, "I feel bad for him."

She nods. "I know, he's a little clueless, isn't he?"

"No, seriously. He's in a new place and he doesn't have any friends."

"And you're going to adopt him?"

I straighten. "Well, why not? I could, I don't know, give him a makeover. Help him fit in."

"Well, if anyone can do it, you can. Though . . ." Her eyebrows wrinkle and I can tell she's thinking about those horrid cords. "Some people are beyond help."

Eden's right. He is a bit of a nightmare. A new outfit might help a bit, but nothing could save him from his swishy way of walking. His too-proper, formal way of speaking. His tendency to spout off obscure fairy lore to anyone who will listen, as easily as if he were chatting about the weather. Though he's human, he's more fairy than anything.

But then it hits me.

Eden's riffling through the magazine rack, looking bored, so she doesn't even notice my eureka moment. At that moment, I see it. It's only a glimmer, but it's there.

The light at the end of the tunnel.

Pip knows everything about fairies. Fairy thoughts. Fairy dreams. Fairy motivations.

Fairy weaknesses.

And he doesn't know it yet, but he's going to tell me them all. He's going to help me find a way to save Cam.

19

I DIDN'T KNOW that five (count 'em, five) chicken gorditas and a Mountain Dew from the Taco Bell at the Menlo Park Mall food court could unleash Pip's wild side. They must not have caffeine in Fairy Land, because he started talking like an auctioneer the moment he wrapped his lips around the straw and took one long, eye-popping swig, and he hasn't shut up yet. From his love for feathered *ewl* (huh?) to his interest in popping *sagmints* (huh? again), it just keeps coming. And I haven't been able to understand a freaking word yet.

"Hold on, hold on. What is an *ewl*?"

He stops midbite. A string of shredded cheese is sticking to his chin. "It's a round object, thrown. Caught. We play with it in the traditional feathered attire."

Warped as it is, it's not entirely unexpected that in the land Pip calls home, they engage in sports dressed like chickens. "You mean, it's a ball?"

He nods brightly. "It can be a vicious game at times. I was quite good at it. . . . Well, being human helped. Fairies don't have much brute strength. They rely on their powers, but use of powers is not allowed during sporting events."

I nod, inspecting him. Pip wouldn't exactly bowl a person over with his muscular physique. In fact, scarecrows have better muscle tone. "And 'popping *sagmints.*' What's that?"

"A *sagmint* is a juicy type of winged creature. You eat it. Popping ones are hot, fresh out of the oven."

"You mean, like roasted turkey?" He nods, mouth full, as I look down and realize that he has polished off all of his gorditas faster than I could finish one sleeve of cinnamon twists.

He is the man of my mother's dreams.

"So," I begin, checking around to see if anyone from our school is watching. So far, the coast is clear. "Humans are better at playing . . . *ewl*, you say. Is there anything else we're better at?"

He thinks for a minute. "No. That's about it."

I can't imagine that we could win Cam back by challenging Massif and Dawn to a game of *ewl*. Especially because I wouldn't be caught dead in feathers. "Don't they have any weaknesses?"

He's looking up at the Taco Bell storefront, studying the menu. "You wouldn't happen to . . ."

"Fine," I sigh, then stand up and head over to the line. When I return with a couple of hard tacos, I warn, "No more."

"Thanks." He grins. "It's just that, fairies don't eat very much. They only eat one meal a day."

"Like dogs?" I don't know why, but that amuses me.

He says, "I have to say, this world is growing on me. I can go wherever I want."

"You can't in Otherworld?"

"Humans can't. They're not exactly welcome in certain places. And there are many rules humans must obey."

"Like?"

"Oh, you know. We can't look directly at a fairy. We have to step aside whenever one is coming toward us."

"Seriously? That's horrible," I say, which only makes me want to bitch-slap Dawn more. "I thought you said they were benevolent to humans."

"They are. Much of the time, they wouldn't bother me. But fairies like to play tricks on humans. Even the kind ones."

"Like, what kinds of tricks?" I ask.

He looks away, then back at me. His lips move, trying to form the words, except nothing comes out. I can tell he isn't interested in talking about it anymore, which makes me think of Mrs. Browne. She'd said he didn't want to talk about his time in Otherworld, which I'd thought was strange, since he talks endlessly about fairy lore in general. What about his past doesn't he want us to know?

"I think we were talking about weaknesses," I say.

"Yes. Right. I can't think of any."

I sigh. "Nothing?"

He takes a bite of his taco and scratches his head, deep in thought, as if he's really trying to help me. It's kind of cute, the faithful-pup routine. As he sits there, scanning the ceiling, I catch a glimpse of a bunch of senior girls leaving Forever 21.

Slumping down in my chair, I inspect him. Then I say, "You know what? I think I'm having a Gap attack. Let's go."

20

I TAKE A gob of styling wax and work it through Pip's hair so that some of it's spiking in all directions like whipped peanut butter and just a bit is falling in his face. It's a big improvement over the slicked-back duck's backside. "Hello, Mr. *GQ*," I say, grinning at him through the mirror in the Brownes' upstairs bathroom.

He looks uncertainly at his reflection and then meets my eyes in the mirror. "*GQ?*"

"It means you're hot." Which, though Pip's ego is in need of boosting, is not a lie. I'd spent a good chunk of the money I'd earned at my summer job on clothes for him. This particular outfit—dark denim jeans, black loafers, and a faded, untucked button-down—would not only put him on the planet, it would possibly qualify him for A-list status.

Mrs. Browne is thrilled. I guess she's happy to see her own flesh and blood looking normal, for once. "It's just amazing," she gushes, inspecting him from all angles.

"Thanks," Pip and I say in unison.

"Morgan, at least let me pay you back for all those clothes. I was planning on taking him shopping myself, once all this . . ." Her voice starts to falter. " . . . is over."

I'm about to say, "Don't worry about it," but she takes one look at Cam and rushes down the hallway, head down, hand clasped over her mouth. I hear a muffled sob before she slams the door to her bedroom.

Cam's face contorts. "She's taking it well."

"I see that. Should you go talk to her?"

"I'd make it worse. She cries every time she looks at me." He starts to gnaw on one of his calluses but then stops and stuffs his hands into his pockets. "But I guess I have that effect on women."

I muss up Pip's hair some more, then undo a button on his collar. "Perfection."

Cam nods at Pip. "Cool, man."

"I'm a genius."

"Whoa, Einstein. There was a lot of room for improvement," he points out.

I say to Pip, "Don't pay any attention to him. I deserve to be adored and thanked profusely. Now, go and put on the heather gray V-neck."

Pip nods and, loyally, scampers across the hall to his room, where the pile of blue Gap bags is lying in the center of his bed. We both stare after him for a minute, and then Cam takes a swig of his Coke.

"How is training going?" I ask, leaning against the bathroom sink. It's getting dark out, and Cam had only poked his head in five minutes ago. Prior to that, the door to his room had been closed, and when I pressed my ear against the door to listen, I couldn't hear a thing. I suppose any normal girl would be jealous of her boyfriend spending hours in a locked bedroom with Barbie, but I've convinced myself that that was only her human form and her true fairy form is decidedly wart-nosed.

"It's going." He sighs. He looks tired and weak, a complete 180 from just a few days ago.

"You look terrible. They're killing you. Why can't you tell them to back off?" I grumble. "Why can't you just say you don't want to go? You don't, do you?"

He bites his lip. "Shh. Of course. But—"

I lean over to wipe a shock of black hair out of his face, and that's when I notice a pink blob hovering over his head. "Yo, Tink," I growl at the air, "isn't there a rainbow somewhere that needs painting?"

The pink blob shivers, and floats into the darkness of the hallway.

"Look," he whispers, his face dark, "I don't have a choice."

"Why not? Because Dawn's always on your back?" I shake my head. "Just tell her to buzz off."

He looks up in the air, then back at me, astonished. "You really can see her."

I nod. "So?"

"So, that baffles me. Humans aren't supposed to see her."

"Well, maybe I'm an extraterrestrial. Or maybe she just sucks at fairy magic."

He flashes a warning look. "Remember what she did to you at school? Be nice. I told her not to touch you, but don't provoke her."

I clench my fists. "You sound like you're on her side."

"No. Listen. I'm not on her side, but I'm not against her, either. She's not evil. She's under orders to bring me back, whatever the costs. My father will kill her if she doesn't obey."

"But you're going to be king."

"I'm not king yet."

I can't believe he's defending the gnat that nearly beat the brains out of me two days ago. I'm about to launch into another argument, but my resolve falters when I look into his eyes. He looks beat. And he's told me before that the way he feels about me won't change. With or without Dawn in his life. "Fine. Sorry." I sigh, feeling bad for being a pest when he obviously has so much more on his mind. He could use a break. "What's our plan for tonight?"

"What?"

"It's Friday. We always go out on Friday."

"I've got a lot of work. They don't think I'm being serious."

"What about tomorrow?"

He takes in a long, slow breath and shakes his head. "Busy."

"This is our last weekend together!" I say, then bite my lip when I realize I'm treading back into pest status.

"I'm so sorry, Boo." Then he whispers, "But you know what we talked about. One, two, three. Always."

I nod. I can feel the tears brimming in my eyes. He reaches over to hug me, and when I pull him close, I whisper, "If we could think of a way out, would you do it?"

He pulls away and looks into my eyes. "Not if it puts you in danger. No way."

"But if it doesn't?"

His voice is resolved. "Of course I would."

I turn and look across the hall, to where Pip is busy pulling the shirt over his head. And I can't help but notice these corded muscles on his upper arms, and gold light from the bedside lamp casting a glow on the curves of his chest. And what are those peeking out above his funky Gap jeans? Washboard abs? Wait. Did a *Men's Health* model sneak in here when I wasn't looking?

Cam is speaking, but I only catch the end of it: "I promise."

I flip my head back to face him. "Um. What?"

"I said to let me work on it. I don't want you getting into any more trouble. You don't know what you're up against. Okay?"

"Uh. Okay." He takes my hand and squeezes it. For the first time I notice that his hands, which have always been covered with calluses from weight lifting, are completely smooth. Smooth, and somehow smaller. My hands don't seem to swim in his, like they used to.

The next time I look, Pip is pulling the sweater over his waist. He looks at me and raises his eyebrows, seeking approval.

"Nice," I sigh.

Cam drops my hand and looks at him. "Cool, but one thing." He takes a pair of shades from his shirt pocket and hands them to Pip. These aren't any ordinary shades; they're the ones I gave Cam last year for his birthday, and he wears them constantly. I used to joke to him that they upped his hotness factor by 1 million percent.

Pip inspects them, then puts them on and looks into the mirror again, with a grin.

And just the slightest bit of confidence.

And that's when I get the first hint that I'm in over my head.

21

IN THE MORNING, I wake trembling from a dream I'd had.

Cam was holding me, tracing his fingers lightly up and down my back like he always does, as if writing a secret message there, and telling me he would never leave me. His voice was a whisper, but a hard one, tangled with worry. And just as I leaned in to kiss him, to take some of that worry away, I realized that it wasn't Cam. It was Pip. It was so real that when I woke, I could still feel the pressure of his lips on mine. His breath was so warm and sweet, and it made me hungry, wanting to meld our bodies together.

After I wash up, I spend a few minutes burying my face in my bath towel, convincing myself that it hadn't actually happened.

But maybe it will? Maybe it's not a dream, but a vision?

Then I spend the next few minutes convincing myself I didn't enjoy it.

What the hell? We're talking about Pencil Box Pip, not a hunk of burning love. Unless, of course, you talk to my mom.

In spite of Cam's warnings, I'd vowed late last night, in between my warped dreams, that even if Dawn killed me, I was going to find a way to save him. Pip's *ewl* discourse hadn't been much help, so at 3 a.m. last night, I went online, reserving every book about fairy lore I could find from the Edison Public Library.

I throw my hair into a ponytail as I head down the stairs, but when I get to the kitchen, I realize something's off. My father is not wearing his white T-shirt and boxers, which is rare for a Saturday morning. That can only mean one thing: company. His familiar chair creaks and moans in protest as he stuffs an entire Boston cream doughnut into his mouth and exclaims, "But she actually was married to his brother!" to someone across the table from him. I figure he must have captured the paperboy or the landscaper. My father will try to carry on a conversation with anyone, even if they show no interest in being spoken to. Even if they're waving a gun in his face, telling him to shut up. But as I come farther into the room, I see our guests. It's Pip and Mrs. Browne. Pip has one hand in a box of Munchkins and is watching my father, rapt. Well, I think he's rapt, but I can't tell for sure, because he still has his sunglasses on.

His face turns toward me and this big, goofy grin spreads across it. I carefully pluck the shades off his nose. "You know these are just for outside, right?"

His eyes widen. He doesn't.

"That's okay. Why are you here?"

My father struggles to pull his belly out from under the

kitchen table. "Oh, hi, Morgan. Our young neighbor and I were just discussing yesterday's *General Hospital*."

"Oh?"

Pip exclaims, "The city of Port Charles sounds interesting."

"You know it's not real."

He squints at me. He doesn't.

"So anyway, why are you here?" I repeat, louder.

His toothy, psychopathic grin hasn't disappeared yet. It totally defeats the purpose of the cool clothes he's wearing. "I have come to be your escort," he says stiffly.

I stare at him. "My what?"

"Cameron said you shouldn't miss the appointment."

"Appointment?"

"There's to be a party next weekend?"

"Yeah, but . . ." I think for a moment and realize that my mom had scheduled the appointment with the Green Toad's events manager for this weekend. It was mainly just to iron out details as to what would be in the buffet line, what color napkins we'd use, et cetera. A week ago, I'd been so excited about it, spending many sleepless hours going back and forth on the tiniest details, like, miniquiches or bacon-wrapped scallops? Teal or silver? In all the commotion, I totally forgot. In fact, I don't care anymore. I have to go on a very important mission to free my boyfriend from a bunch of overrated mosquitoes. Plus, teal and silver are my colors, but either one would look bad with my destined-to-be-nightmarish complexion. "That's today?"

My mom comes in, fastening a gold stud to her ear. "Don't tell me you forgot!"

"I forgot."

She shakes her head and puts a hand on Mrs. Browne's

{105}

shoulder. "*Marone!* These kids! Can you believe she went on for days about this party, and she forgets?"

Mrs. Browne says nothing but gives me a look that says she completely understands. From the way she's shifting in her chair, I think a party is the last thing on her mind, too.

I shrug like the ungrateful brat my mother thinks I am.

"I think it's very nice for this young man to offer to come with us, especially since Cam is . . ." She looks at him. "Where did you say Cam is?"

Pip says simply, "Studying the fairy ways," as he stuffs an entire jelly doughnut in his face. It's like he and my father are in an eating contest.

When she looks at me, I explain, "It's an elective. I took creative writing instead."

Her questioning look slowly disintegrates, and she grabs her coat. "Well, that's fine. We need a man's opinion. Shall we be off?"

Reluctantly, I follow her out the door, contemplating that. Pip is human, so I guess he is more of a man than Cam is. But when I turn around, I see that this "manly specimen" has a gigantic blob of jelly on his upper lip.

And the irony of it is, in fairy logic, Cam's the one who doesn't belong here.

I'VE ONLY BEEN to the city a handful of times, so as my mother navigates the streets, it appears like we're going in circles. Each building is taller than the next, bearing down on me, making it difficult to breathe. When we arrive at the Green Toad, I want to sit down and bury my head between my knees. The lush décor—toads dancing on the walls, primitive cave drawings, and gigantic urns filled with tropical flowers of every color—something I once found funky and eclectic, now just bothers me. My mother begins to talk to a water-goblet filler as if he already knew who she is. As if my event isn't one of hundreds they put on every year.

"Mom," I mumble, trying to hide my aggravation, since I

know she's going to all this effort for me, "maybe we should talk to the lady we talked to on the phone?"

Luckily, before I can spear her with one of the tribal artifacts nearby, a pale, matronly lady with a huge mouth and way-too-red lipstick greets us and introduces herself as the receptionist. She leads us into another room, which is wallpapered with even more dancing frogs. Maybe it's because they're so happy, maybe it's because last time I was here, Cam pretended to be one and cracked me up doing a Kermit impersonation that sounded like Donald Duck, but all I can think about is getting out.

Instead, I sit in an overstuffed chair covered with fabric splashed with orange and green palm trees and stare down at a rainbow of napkin swatches while my mother babbles on. Something about how she hopes that the water fountain in the lobby, which isn't working today, will be fully operational by Friday. Mrs. Browne just sits there, a blank look on her face, as if she's at a funeral. After another ten minutes, my mom finally turns to me and says, "Well?"

"Um. What?"

"The napkins," she grumbles, jabbing her finger at the swatches.

Sighing, I say, "I give up. I have no decision."

My mother grinds her teeth. "You'd better have a decision."

Whenever I think about this party now, I think about doom. And it became so much more real the second we arrived in the city and walked through the huge, arched doors to the Green Toad. A month ago, Cam and I were at this very place, choosing songs we wanted the DJ to play, talking about what we'd wear, bursting with excitement. But now, there's a fifty-pound weight on my chest. The night of our sixteenth birthday is no longer party time. It's D-day.

Still, the parents are spending a lot of money on this, so I can't appear ungrateful. I force a smile and say, "I'm fine with either."

My mother's eyes narrow. "Well, you definitely had an opinion last week." Which is true; life seemed a whole lot simpler then. She takes the book from my hands and says, "You liked the silver. Or the teal. Make a decision."

"I—I can't." Is this what a mental breakdown feels like?

Mrs. Browne, who has not said a word since we left my house, finally pipes up. "You take your time, hon."

I give her a grateful smile. "Which do you like?"

"They're both very pretty."

Some help she is.

"I like this," Pip says, scraping the bottom of a plate with a fork, oblivious to the napkin upheaval. For the first time, I notice that there are half-full plates of appetizers and desserts in front of us. Half-full, because Pip has already eaten just about everything that is within reaching distance of his chair. There are about five empty paper plates in his lap. Thankfully, he's stopped short of licking them. "What is this called?"

"Whipped cream?" the events manager says, giving me an amused, "Is he for real?" look. Her name is Gizelle and she's so completely put together, with her four-inch heels, crisp white blouse, and French twist, that she looks at least thirty. But when she flashes Pip a coy smile, and gnaws on her lower lip, she's reduced to my age. I've seen that look on many a girl's face around Cam. It's subtle, but I've become an expert on it.

She's *flirting* with him.

Wait. She's getting all hot and bothered over a guy who gets more food on his mouth than in it?

My mother grins at Pip like he is the son she never had and giggles something about growing boys.

I glare at her, annoyed. It's amazing how a new outfit and a little hair gel can turn grown women into Jell-O. Are we really that shallow? "Um, silver. Okay."

"Silver it is. Oh, but the teal is so . . . What do you think, Pip?" my mother asks, putting a hand on his knee as I start to groan. "It's always nice to have a man's opinion."

He looks at me and, without missing a beat, says, "I agree with Morgan."

For once, I'm grateful to have him around.

"So, it's settled. Silver it is." She takes the swatch and folds it neatly in front of Gizelle. "Now, you were going to give us a tour of that lovely courtyard? The balcony is beautiful. All that ivy!"

Mrs. Browne is the first to stand. She looks almost as green as the frogs on the wall, so I think she needs some air. Gizelle stands and smooths her hair, then checks to see if Pip is noticing. He isn't; he's busy studying some tribal masks on the wall behind her desk. Though she's a hottie, I get the feeling Pip wouldn't notice her if her hair were on fire. He's so busy trying to navigate this strange new world that he's probably the only sixteen-year-old guy who *doesn't* think constantly about sex.

That's probably why I can't help wanting to tell Gizelle to back off. Pip is naïve and unsure of himself, and he needs protection from this cruel world.

Pouting, she gives up and turns toward a corridor. "This way."

"You know, Mom," I say, standing, "you guys go ahead. I just want to check out the room again."

Gizelle says, "There's a dance class going on in there now, but feel free to look around."

Pip says, "I think I will stay with Morgan."

My mother and Gizelle let out a collective sigh, and I half expect Gizelle to let her hair down and lick her lips as a last-ditch attempt to get him to notice her. She doesn't; they just head off, their heels click-clicking in chorus on the parquet floor.

"What is this event for?" Pip asks me when we're alone.

"Our sixteenth birthday. Turning sixteen is a big deal here," I explain, twisting a lock of my hair.

"It's a big deal where I come from, too."

"Really? Do they have wild parties in Fairy Land?"

"Well, yes, often. But what I mean is that, for a fairy, their sixteenth birthday is their Becoming."

"Oh, right. Becoming."

"Yes, on a fairy's sixteenth birthday, they become a true fairy. Right now, Cameron's a—"

"Larva. I get it. So Dawn is a full fairy. Is she older than sixteen?"

He fiddles with a zipper on the new jacket I bought him. "She is forty-three."

"Wait. What?" I can't help but feel disgusted. "So he's marrying my mother. Gross."

"Fairy life spans are much longer than human lives. A fairy will live a thousand years. So in that way, they are very close in age."

"All right, but if they have such long life spans, why are they in such a rush to take him away from me on my sixteenth birthday? Can't they wait a couple of years? Maybe until I'm eighty and toothless?"

He says, "The only time, other than on the day of his birth, that the portal to cross into Otherworld will be open for Cameron is at midnight on his Becoming. You see, it's easy to come to this world. It's nearly impossible to go back to Otherworld."

"So until then, he's stuck here?"

"The door isn't open."

"And after that . . ."

"It will never be open again."

"But Dawn—"

"There are some exceptions to the rule. As his chosen guide, only Dawn can transcend the barrier with him. She is the only one with this ability. Very powerful."

"Yes, Dawn is wonderful," I mumble, grabbing him by his sleeve. "Come on."

I lead him down a hallway, to double doors with a placard over them that says TAHITI ROOM. I grasp a gilded handle and push a heavy, ornately carved door open, and we squeeze inside as Sinatra croons, *"Just the way you look tonight."*

This is where, in the movies, the needle of the record player would screech off its track. Twelve gray-haired ladies are staring at us. Six pairs of women, standing, midwaltz, in their Sunday best. The smell of Jean Naté, the perfume my grandmother used to have a vat of in her bathroom, burns my nostrils, even from a distance.

A fit, well-endowed lady in a short blond bob, who is considerably younger than the rest and wearing a hot-pink leotard, bounds over to us, her chest doing its own salsa dance. "Oh, wonderful."

"We're here to—"

"Don't be shy. We welcome all ages here."

I'm not exactly sure where "here" is, but I take a step back, because it's definitely not someplace I want to be. "No, we just wanted to—"

"You're just in time." She smiles gratefully, then leans in and whispers, "I was wanting to shake things up a bit. You game?"

Uh-oh. This cannot be good. I look at Pip, who is nodding very cordially at the ladies. They giggle, too, just like my mom. What *is* this strange effect he has on women?

The fit lady claps her hands. "Tango. And this young couple is going to demonstrate."

Yes, she is pointing at us. I feel the half bite of miniquiche I'd tasted in Gizelle's office trying to force its way up my throat. "We can't—"

She claps again. "Don't tell me you can't. I'll show you. Now, get into position."

I feel her adjusting my limbs like I'm some life-sized Barbie, placing Pip's arm around my waist. He pulls me in close, and I don't think I've ever been this near to a guy that wasn't Cam, so maybe that's the reason I start to feel hot and feverish. Or maybe it's because if it isn't solo butt-shaking or hug-and-sway, I don't dance. Pip is grinning dumbly at me, so it's obvious he has no idea what he's in for. I feel his arm around my back, pulling me into the curve of his body, his cool, soft hand wrapped perfectly around mine. And he's so close I can smell something of him, something other than the Jean Naté, something familiar, but my mind is racing and I can't concentrate enough to know what it is. All I know is that this is so wrong, and it is time to leave.

"Listen," I mutter, as I realize the old ladies are forming a half circle around us. I think one of them is pointing out to another how my jeans are too tight. "We just came here to check out the room. I don't know how to tango."

Fit Lady looks deflated for a moment, but only for a moment. She brightens up with, "It's very simple. Just follow my cues and you'll be pros in no time!"

Before I can protest, she jogs over to a little radio and pops in a new CD. Immediately, slow, seductive Latin music fills the air. The drumbeat pulsates with my own heartbeat.

I am going to faint.

"And one, and two, and . . ."

I decide that the man should have the responsibility of leading, so I won't do anything. I will just stand there and let myself be taken like a rag doll. Then, hopefully, when the two of us have fallen into a disgusting mangled heap of broken limbs, Mrs. I-Can-Conquer-the-World will give up trying to teach us. I clamp my eyes shut and let my mind go blank, bracing for the pain I'll feel when my body hits the parquet floor.

We begin to move. I feel the air on my face, and my limbs are being pulled every which way in what feel like short, jerky movements. It feels like I'm having a convulsion, so I know we can't be doing it right. Can we?

Then I hear Fit Lady cry, "Good. Good!"

So I have to open my eyes. I see Pip, concentrating hard on the instructor's footsteps, and he's following them, pulling me along with him. We're perfectly in beat with the music. Amazingly, I see the mouths of the old ladies curved into mesmerized Os over their dentures. We're doing it right.

When I feel comfortable enough that he's not going to trip me, I manage to look down, and see that his feet are gliding gracefully on the floor in his black loafers. He's even doing this very hot rhythmic figure eight with his hips.

Maybe it's the music that's growing on me, or maybe it's that I'm giddy from not having had anything to eat except half a miniquiche, but after a moment or so, I start to move my hips, too. And suddenly, I'm breathless again, but in a good way.

Once Pip gets into the groove, he stops looking at the instructor and his eyes fasten on mine. So close like this, they're shocking in their brilliance, so light blue as to be almost white. Like silver medallions moving back and forth on a chain, they're hypnotizing. Where did they come from? I swear they weren't so beautiful a day ago, when we were sitting in the food court, talking about *ewl* and popping *sagmints*.

"Where did you learn to do this?" I whisper in his ear, still unable to break from his gaze.

"Fairies love to dance. This is similar to one of theirs," he explains as he slows to a near stop. His eyes focus on Fit Lady again, and before I can ask what he's doing, he expertly glides his leg out from underneath his body, dragging his foot on the ground.

"Yours should follow his," Fit Lady says, watching my legs.

"Like how?" I ask, suddenly nervous again. I pull one out from under me and clumsily lean it against his, nearly stepping on his toe. "Like this?"

Then I notice Pip is back to staring at me, and self-consciousness washes over me. And heat stings my cheeks. I'm blushing, something I never, ever do.

"I meant the other one, but okay." Disappointment hangs in her voice.

"Oh, sorry," I mumble, upset that she doesn't have the same faith in my dancing abilities as she has in Pip's.

Then I feel her hand on my leg, pulling it up into the air. I toddle about on one leg like a top that's about to fall, so Pip steadies me, and I hold on so tight to his arms with my sweaty hands as to cut off his circulation. But he doesn't seem to mind. I watch as she grips my leg at the knee and pulls it, higher, higher . . . almost to Pip's hip level, then forces me to extend and curve it around him. Ow, I am not a pretzel. "What are you doing?"

"*Gancho*," she says. "Just take your leg up and wrap it around his body."

"Wait. Wh-wh-at?"

He's still staring at me with those amazing eyes as I push him away, falling back onto my elbows with a deafening crack.

23

"I FEEL TERRIBLE," Pip says to me as he helps me up to my bedroom.

That's exactly what I was thinking.

My mother spent most of the ride home from the city hospital complaining about how wearing an Ace bandage on my arm would ruin all of my sweet-sixteen pictures, and as we pulled into the driveway, she was still hurling Italian curses at me loud enough to wake our ancestors in Sicily. She refused to look at me after she turned off the ignition; instead, she wordlessly retired to the living room to catch the end of *MacGyver* with my dad. The silent treatment is a favorite tool in my mom's arsenal; however, since she loves talking as much as she loves food, I fully expect her to be chattering away by tomorrow morning.

Until then, peace. Just what I need.

"Leave the door open," I instruct Pip, and then feel the need to explain, as if he has any clue what I mean, "My mother's strict Italian upbringing."

"Oh." He nods with understanding and does exactly as he's told, as usual.

Though I'd only bruised my arm, every part of my body feels like it's been through a meat grinder. My left arm is worse, but both are swollen and purple from wrist to elbow, and my lower spine feels like it might snap apart.

"There's nothing you could have done. It's all my stupid fault," I tell him as he fluffs some pillows on my bed and gingerly lays me down. He's so careful that I know he isn't just saying it; he really does feel terrible about the whole thing.

"No. Cameron told me to look out for you."

"He did?" I stop pulling the covers over my body and sigh. Before I can be overcome with an urge to smother myself with a pillow over losing the best boyfriend in the world, I say, "That's because he knows I'll never be able to make it without him. I'm hopeless."

"He told me he thinks you're the bravest girl he's ever met."

I raise my eyebrows and then sigh. Yes, maybe I used to be. Having the world's yummiest boyfriend and being able to predict the future would boost anyone's confidence. But now that the yummy boyfriend is leaving me forever, and my amazing psychic abilities can't do a thing to stop it . . . suddenly I feel like I'm walking a tightrope without a net. "Maybe I was, once. Not so much anymore. Sometimes I think I'd rather jump off a cliff than face a day without him."

He looks surprised. "Is it normal for humans to feel that way when they're in love?"

I shrug and nod, then study him. He really does have no idea. Then I roll over and prop myself up with my good elbow. "Why? Haven't you ever been in love?"

He looks away. "In Otherworld, that love doesn't exist."

"Oh, right. Dawn said something about that before. That Cam couldn't possibly love me. So fairies aren't supposed to fall in love?"

He opens his mouth and closes it again. "In Otherworld, a fairy does not love one person above all others."

"Well, talk about horrible." I shake my head, suddenly feeling dreamy and warm and altogether touchy-feely from the medication. I guess that's why I launch into a heart-to-heart with Pip. "But what about you? You're human. You've never been in love?"

He looks away. I can tell I'm making him uncomfortable, treading into that part of Otherworld that he just doesn't seem interested in talking about. I'm about to change the subject, when he softly answers, "I'm not sure if I can be that kind of person. Or if anyone could feel that way about me."

I smile, thinking how oblivious he must be to not have noticed the events manager crushing on him earlier today. And when he danced with me, he could have passed for more than just human . . . girls would have found him downright droolworthy. "Well, I think someone could feel that way about you. I mean, anything's possible, right? Cam is a fairy. He isn't supposed to love me. But he does."

He nods but doesn't say anything.

"Why don't you ask a girl to our party next Friday? I bet one would go with you, now," I press on, biting my tongue with the urge to finish that sentence with "that you don't look like a goober."

His bottom lip quivers. "Uh, no. I wouldn't know what to do."

"Just go up to one on Monday in school and say, 'Listen, there's a party on Friday, and let's go together.' That's it."

"That's it?"

"Yeah, it's easy. But pick a cute girl. Aim high. You're totally worth it," I cheerlead, then realize that maybe the Percocet is kicking in a little too nicely.

Still, he gets this inspired gleam in his eyes. "Well, okay. Maybe I will."

Yawning, I say, "You just need the right girl to fall in love with. I was lucky to find the right guy as early as I did."

"So you know that Cameron is your true love?"

"I'm positive."

He clears his throat. "In that case, there's something you should know."

He sounds so serious that I lean in, wondering all the time if it's going to be an Edenism, like, "I have ten toes!" or "The sky is blue." "What?"

"We have to be very quiet, or else," he whispers, those clear eyes piercing mine. "But I know a way to keep Cameron here with you."

24

NOW I'M SITTING on the front porch, in darkness, waiting for Cam. There's a baby cricket in one of the rosebushes, and I can see its new, wet wings glistening in the yellow streetlight. I wonder if that's how Cam feels, struggling to keep up with the parts of his body that are so new and unfamiliar.

After Pip left, I'd tried to go to sleep, thinking it would be easy, since the painkiller had made me so wonky I could barely stand. Instead, fueled by what Pip had told me, my mind kicked into overdrive, assembling a giant jigsaw puzzle, fitting each piece together until I sprang from my bed, forgetting the pain of my bruised arm, and called Cam to tell him to meet me outside, stat.

It is possible.

I hear the creak of his screen door, and, realizing I've been so excited that I completely forgot to primp, I smooth back my hair and wipe any errant toothpaste from the corners of my mouth.

"Hey, Boo," Cam says, coming through the bushes. One half of his hair, the side he sleeps on, is spiked, standing straight on end like the bristles of a comb. His face looks puffy, and there are dark circles under his eyes, not much different from the black gunk he puts on before each game. He looks at my arm. "Damn. Pip told me."

He leans over to give me a kiss, but before he can, I burst out with, "So you talked to Pip?"

He blinks, surprised. "A little. Why? What is this about?"

I cock my head toward the garage and whisper, "I think my dad's up. Can we take a walk?"

He nods and says, loudly, "Okay, let's take a walk, and you can tell me everything I missed at the . . . at the meeting of the . . . oh, screw it. Sorry, Mr. Sparks."

A second later, there's the sound of movement, the noise of metal against metal, and shuffling. But I'm focusing my attention on Cam. Though he's a terrible liar, he is usually never at a loss for words. Not like this. While my dad huffs up the staircase inside with the last of his dignity, I say, "Things are bad?"

"What do you think?" He pulls me from the stoop with both hands.

I dig my feet into my flip-flops and stand up to face him. I stick out my chin, shrink down. Stand on my tiptoes. "You've . . ."

"Lost a few inches. Yeah. And get a load of this." He turns and pulls up his T-shirt, and in the small slash of light, I can see that there are rips in the bandages, and this greenish, black-veined scale is poking through. I try swallow the disgust, but it doesn't look pretty or soft or nice, like fairy parts should look. It looks like a gigantic fly wing. And the lump on his back is now twice as big as it once was. He faces me, eyes full. "I am officially a freak."

I take him by the hand, and we walk down my driveway, into the street. Everything is silent and still save for a few crickets and frogs and the tat-tat-tat of our neighbor's automatic sprinkler. I pull a plastic bag and a rubber band out from the pocket of my sleep pants. "I have something amazing to tell you. Let's go for a swim."

As I'm fastening the plastic over my arm with the band, he looks across the street and mutters, "Can you reverse this?"

"No, but I can—"

"Then I don't want to know," he sighs, running his hands through his hair. "I don't want to get wet. I'm tired, and I'm going back to bed."

As I mentioned, he's a total Mr. Grouchy Pants when he doesn't get enough sleep. I grab him by the elbow and push him toward the sprinkler. "Trust me. You're going to feel a zillion percent better when I tell you this."

"If I've told you once, I've told you a million times. Don't exaggerate."

I'm happy for the old Cam humor, until I see the glower on his face. Still, he digs his hands into his pockets and follows me.

In the cool early-October air, the drops soak clear through to my bones. The sprinkler is the kind that slowly moves around, spreading water as it goes, then returns fast, like a typewriter. I grab him and we walk in time with it, then race back to the beginning when it returns. I say, "Remember how we did this when we were kids?"

He stops and faces me, emotionless, his hair matted against his eyes, so that I can barely see them. It melts into his black eyes and stubble, so that his face is just one big mess of darkness and despair. "Your point?"

I keep running in a circle, like a two-year-old, hoping he'll catch the fever. "Just reminiscing."

He scowls. "I don't want to reminisce. I am free-eez-in-g." He whines the last word as if it had four syllables, with a big "guh" at the end.

"Okay, okay." I stop and collapse on the ground, running my Popsicle toes through the wet grass. I try to keep it a whisper, just in case, but my excitement gets to be too much for me. "Pip said there *is* a way to keep you here!"

He is silent. First, he looks up at the sky, and for once I can't tell what he's thinking. He gnaws his lip, then walks toward me, finally falling on his knees beside me. "Yeah?"

"Yes!" I say, grabbing him by the neck. "Pip is ninety-nine percent sure that it will work. And you and I will be together, just like we planned."

He looks into my eyes, and looks away, like he needs more reassuring. "But is it—"

"Yes. Totally safe." Well, nothing is totally safe. But it's close. "See? Everything is going to work out."

He doesn't speak for a long time. "It is? Did you envision it?"

I catch my breath, shocked that he would ask. He has never, ever wanted to know his future before. But maybe that was when my predictions involved who would win the next football game. This is more serious. This is his life. Our life. I'm quiet for a moment, knowing that the longer I pause, the less truthful I'll appear. Quickly, I force the words out, so that they tumble over one another. "Yes. And you know my visions are always right."

I'm still dwelling on the lie, feeling its bitter taste on my tongue and wondering if it will come back to haunt me later, when he says, "Why? Why would you want to be with me? I'm going to be a freak. Nothing can stop this."

"I've always thought you were a freak," I say, grinning down at him as he puts his head in my lap. In the moonlight, he's more beautiful than ever; his face looks cut from marble, his lips look smooth and kissable, and the bit of light brings out the speckles of brown in his normally black eyes. Breathing heavy, he lets the water hit his face, unmoving, like a statue. I stroke my hand through his wet hair, over his grizzled jawline, and lean over to give him a kiss. "And you're right about one thing. Nothing can stop this."

25

I'M SITTING AT my desk, eating a Hot Pocket and trying to scrape a smear of tomato sauce off my homework, when my mother opens the door a crack. Without knocking, of course. I'm about to launch into my standard "Hello? Privacy!" rant, but she's already talking loud enough for the entire neighborhood to hear. "We received a call this morning from Mrs. Nelson. She wanted to thank me for the *sfogliatelle*, and inform me that some young lady I might know was"—and she whispers this part, though even her whisper is louder than regular speech—"fornicating on her front lawn?"

"We weren't. . . . I mean, seriously," I blubber, so mortified I can barely hold my pencil. "She's been watching too much late-night cable. I just had an urge to . . . play in the sprinklers."

As the excuse leaves my mouth, I am fully aware of how dumb it sounds.

"At one in the morning?"

I shrug. "Serves her right for watering her lawn in October. She needs to let it go."

She rolls her eyes. "She probably forgot to turn off the automatic setting. Mrs. Nelson is going through a very trying time, what with poor Gracie."

"Is Gracie any better?" I ask, grateful to sway the conversation away from our late-night improprieties. I mean, seriously, adults can so overreact.

"No. Mrs. Nelson told me it will be any day now."

"Oh, that's horrible. Maybe your *sfogliatelle* will help bring a miracle," I say, though I truly doubt it. I'm just being angelic in hopes of cleansing her of the mental image of her only child doing the nasty on the front lawn.

"Maybe," she says. She continues to stare at the ground, lost in thought.

"I have homework," I finally say, hoping to nudge her out the door. "Anything else?"

"Oh." She opens the door a little more, and I see Pip standing there. He's wearing another Gap outfit, and it's cute to see that he really has been making an effort to muss up his hair the way I taught him to.

"Good," I say, leaning over and pulling him into the room.

"I'll just leave you two alone," my mother says, beaming. And, get this, she actually closes the bedroom door behind her! Now, she's never had anything against Cam, but why is she so head-over-heels for Pip? Is it because Cam oozes sex, and Pip carries the Good Mothering Seal of Approval on his forehead?

I'm still contemplating this when I realize he's fidgeting. "Sit down. We have work to do."

He glances at my bed, which is the only open seat in my room, and then, bashful, Indian-squats on the rug.

I pull the paper off my desk and wave it in front of him. "Voilà. I wrote everything out to make sure we're all clear."

"Does Cameron know about this?"

Last night, despite his protests, I'd managed to convince Cam that I would love him no matter what and that staying with me, no matter how he looked, was better than leaving. He agreed wholeheartedly that he didn't want to leave me, but his big concern was that I would drop him because of a few silly wings. As if I were that shallow. I nod and say, "But Dawn is always on his back, so he can't help us. It's up to us to save him."

Pip swallows. Then he swallows again. His face is turning red. Pip is not used to defying authority. Hell, he probably isn't used to defying *anyone.*

"Don't be afraid. You said yourself"—and I read from the paper—"'A fairy must cross over to Otherworld of his own free will.' And he doesn't want to."

He opens his mouth, closes it, then opens it again, like a guppy gasping for air outside of its bowl. "They will be angry if he doesn't go."

"So what? We had nothing to do with his decision. It's totally up to him," I explain, watching his ears turn the color of lobsters. "And besides, what can they do?"

According to Pip, at a fairy's Becoming, the portal will open at midnight and will not close until a young life has crossed into Otherworld. But the fairy must go of their own free will. There have been stories of humans accidentally crossing into the portal before the fairy could make it across, leaving the poor fairy stranded in this world. So if, by some strange twist of fate, someone else takes Cam's place, he will be forced to stay here. With me. Forever.

I like the sound of that.

"They will be angry," he repeats. "I am not sure what they will do."

"What happened to the other fairies in the stories you spoke of? The ones who were stranded in this world?"

He says, "I do not know. They were never heard from again."

"Oh. Still, it's worth a try."

"But remember: somebody has to go in his place, or otherwise the portal will remain open and the balance between Otherworld and this world will be destroyed. There's a legend that says if the balance is ever upset, both worlds will be thrown into turmoil, consumed by fire for a thousand years."

I raise my eyebrows. "Seriously?"

He nods.

I imagine the guilt I'd feel knowing my stupid boyfriend-saving plan was the sole source of our world's global warming crisis. Leaning back in my chair, I say, "Okay, right, we can just substitute some other poor sucker."

Pip whispers, "It's important that they not find out about this. Dawn's only objective is to convince him to return to Otherworld, and I do not know how far she would go to remove the barriers in her way."

"You're talking about me."

"Yes."

"Like what? Turning me into a horse?"

I'm only half joking, but he nods like it's a serious possibility. I stamp out the feeling of nausea that's beginning in my stomach.

"Relax," I whisper, more to myself than to him. "By the time they realize that he doesn't want to go, it will be too late. I've told Cam to just play it cool, act like he's really into being a fairy, and then, at the last minute, he can pretend like he had a change of heart. And by then, Dawn won't have the time to do anything to convince him."

He nods, but I can tell he's still uneasy. Finally, he says, "We won't be able to protect the . . . the 'poor sucker' she takes with her, though."

"I know," I say solemnly, thinking about how we could possibly make Sara Phillips, the way-too-peppy and beautiful captain of the cheerleaders, enter into the portal on his behalf. Promise a free pedicure? "She—I mean, whoever it is—will be our sacrifice."

He takes a deep breath and looks at the ground. "I think I may have failed to mention this. The person Dawn takes with her . . . it has to be someone who is also turning sixteen on October fifteenth."

I nearly fall out of my chair. "What?"

"Um, yes. Humans, too, can only cross into Otherworld on either their day of birth or their sixteenth birthday. No other time."

His eyes are wide, as if he's afraid of me. Me. So I quiet my voice and calmly say, "Why didn't you tell me this before?"

"I don't know. I . . ."

I think for a minute, about our entire high school class. Nope, out of everybody, it's only Cam and I who are October 15 birthdays. And it's not like I'm going to sacrifice my life on Earth just to keep Cam here; that would be defeating the purpose of this glorious plan to save true love. So what can I do? Advertise on MySpace to see if I can get any poor soon-to-be-sweet-sixteens to come to our party? Take out an ad on Craigslist?

Hopeless.

"This is a major problem. I don't know anyone else who was born on the same day Cam and I were." I sigh.

"Yes, you do." He gulps. Then he gulps again. "Me."

"I CAN DO it," he says, his voice unwavering. For the first time, as he kneels in front of me, he looks rather strong and substantial, like a knight readying for battle. "I am not afraid. I've lived there before, and I can do it again."

I shake my head. Pip is a good guy, strange as he may be. He didn't deserve the cruelty of the fairies the first time, and he certainly doesn't deserve a second helping. "But you said that they treated humans badly there. They were mean to you."

He leans toward me, his eyes turning dark gray, then plucks at the carpet. "But do I really fit in here?"

It's true that he's a bit of an oddball. But in a good way. It's obvious he doesn't see himself, doesn't see that his differences make him interesting, not an outcast, like he was in Otherworld.

A few days ago, I was laughing with the others about the new kid, but now I see that this "freak" is a faithful, good person. A person who doesn't deserve to be treated badly . . . by anyone. "You fit in among those that matter."

He picks at his shirt. "Just because of these new clothes?"

"You didn't need those. You were fine the way you were. I was just being superficial."

He leans back, and at that moment I see a hint of the broad curve of his chest behind his Gap tee. There are thick muscles in his forearms that rival even Cam's, and I swear they weren't there before. When he says, "I look at it as doing my part, for true love," I almost can't remember whose love he's talking about.

When there's a knock on the door, I mumble a "yeah?" toward the hallway, taking for granted that it's my mother delivering some freshly made snacks.

The door opens, and instead, standing there with her hands on her hips is my worst nightmare. Dawn has shape-shifted into her model form again and is wearing a patchwork-quilt dress that she manages to make look runway chic instead of Holly Hobbie. She tosses a glare in Pip's direction, and immediately, he tenses and bows his head in respect.

I can't breathe. How long has she been out there? Did she hear?

"Oh, good," I say, putting on my bravest face and standing so that I'm at eye level with her. "To what do we owe the pleasure?"

If she had heard anything, she isn't letting on. Instead, she smiles sweetly and points at Pip. "I need that human," she announces, as if he's a roll of toilet paper. "Cameron needs one to practice on."

I cross my arms over my chest. "To practice what, exactly?"

Pip doesn't seem to care. "Yes, right away," he says, scurrying to his feet.

I hold him back with my arm. "You're not going to turn him into anything, are you?"

She laughs. "If we do, we always turn him back."

I shake my head at her. I don't care what Cam thinks. She is so, so evil. Then, I say, "He'll be with you in a minute," and slam the door in her face.

When I turn to Pip, his ears are red again, as if his head might explode. "You shouldn't have . . ."

"She'll get over it," I say, waving the thought of her away with my hand. "I just wanted to ask you . . . What you said before . . . about true love . . . Do you really mean it?"

He nods.

I study his face. He's completely serious. "I don't know why you would make that sacrifice for me. Are you sure?"

He nods again, more firmly. "It's not a big sacrifice. I've lived there for sixteen years."

I don't know how he can think it, but I am glad he does. Because he's the key, my only hope of keeping Cam with me. I gave him some Gap clothes, and he's giving me this. Either he's a total sucker when it comes to making bargains, or there's something to it that I'm missing.

"Thank you." I move next to him and cautiously wrap my arms around him. It starts as an awkward hug, but as I press against him, feeling the muscles of his arms around my shoulders, his chest pressed against my body, I have a hard time releasing him. As I sit there with him on my pink shag carpet, knowing the embrace has gone on for too long to be merely friendly but unable to do anything about it, I notice something. A scent, ever so faint, but familiar. The scent I'd caught among the perfumed old ladies at the Toad but had been unable to identify. This time, I recognize it immediately.

A scent like the woods. And barbershop aftershave.

27

THAT NIGHT, I go to sleep bitter and heartbroken. Bitter because I haven't seen Cam all day. He'd promised to come by after dinner but never showed and then called me at nine to say he was too tired. And heartbroken because I long desperately for the days before this nightmare started.

I miss the old, easygoing, self-assured Cam. This new version hates who he is and what he is becoming, so much so that he can't even disguise those feelings with jokes anymore. When I told him that he should at least come over for a little, that maybe we could just crash and watch a little TV, he refused, because "I need a lot of rest to complete this transformation into full freak status."

I climb into bed, thinking about the party, and the plan to

keep him here, and wondering what type of life Cam will have in this world as a fairy. How small will he get? He's already lost about six inches and twenty pounds, and—who knows, since I haven't seen him all day—he's probably lost more by now. I can't very well picture him playing college football at a Big East school, like he'd planned. And how much will those wings get in the way? He's always talked about either being a weatherman or working on Wall Street. I can't imagine him flying from place to place with a three-piece suit and briefcase.

All his life, Cam was the perfect one. Everything came easily to him. The newspaper said it best: "Cam Browne can do anything."

But that was then. That was the old Cam.

I'm not so sure the new Cam will be able to handle this.

But he has to, because I can't handle life without him.

I kick off the covers, pop in some more Enya, and sit cross-legged on my bed, then close my eyes. "Fluffernutter," I murmur.

There's a piece of stray hair from my ponytail tickling my nose, muddling my concentration, so it takes a while before I actually see the aquamarine ripples of water in the pool. When I'm lost in them, I whisper, "Show me Cam Browne."

The waves turn fuzzy, and then . . .

Nothing.

Complete blackness.

I sit there for a moment, waiting, until I lose patience. "Show me Cam Browne," I say, louder.

Either my vision is of him hanging out in a closet, or I got nothing.

"Cameron Browne?" I ask, giving the side of my head a thwack.

Hopeless.

I take a deep breath. Must find my Zen.

Relaxing, not completely but just enough so that my heart isn't pounding out of my chest, I go back to my *Fluffernutters*. When the ripples appear, I say, "Show me Pip Merriweather."

The ripples part, the clouds clear, and an image begins to come to light.

Yeah, I still got it.

But the celebration comes to a rapid halt when I enter the vision.

MY DREAMS THAT night, again, are filled with visions of Cam and Pip. I'm in my bed, Cam is there, and once again, he's kissing me, his weight pressing into me. His hands are tangled in my hair, working through it, and I feel his breath on my skin as his tongue trails down my neck. I sigh, closing my eyes, because it feels so amazing. When he pulls the straps of my tank top down around my shoulders, his lips trailing across my collarbone, I can only think that I want him to keep this going, forever. When I finally open my eyes and peer past my chin, I see a head of peanut-butter-blond hair. *It isn't Cam,* I tell myself. *You know who it is.* I know it is wrong.

And yet, I don't tell him to stop.

I wake that morning with my sheets knotted around my legs,

feeling like the worst girlfriend on earth. I quickly throw on some clothes and race downstairs and out the door before my mother can pose her "Orange juice?" question. I find Pip standing at the line between our houses, backpack slung over both shoulders, inspecting either the grass or his toes. He's wearing another Gap special, this time a hooded sweatshirt, baggy jeans, and sneakers, his toughest, most gangsta ensemble yet. It serves to make him slightly more threatening than the Keds-wearing Pip, but still very vanilla.

And yet, when he looks up and meets my eyes, I have to turn away. Is dream cheating really cheating? No. I have dreams that I'm naked in school sometimes, and that doesn't mean that I want to be naked. A dream about Pip doesn't mean I want him. Of course, I can still feel his hands in my hair, his breath on my . . .

Damn. Focus, girl.

I cannot be having these feelings. They're ridiculous. Even though he's ditched the cords, he's still Pencil Box Pip. I have the most perfect boyfriend in this world, and in any other world, for that matter.

Pip senses my minor mental breakdown. How can he not? I bet I even smell guilty. "Is there a problem?" he asks.

Cam is nowhere in sight, and I'm glad. I can't face him.

I take a deep breath and mentally chant, *Cam is my true love, Cam is my true love, Cam is my true love,* a few times. Then I force myself back to the issue at hand, the real issue, the vision I'd had before I'd gone to bed. "Major. Last night, before I went to sleep, I had a vision of you."

He raises his eyebrows. "Are you an enchantress?"

"A what?" I wrinkle my nose, but the truth is, "enchantress" sounds kind of nice. "Um, no. Just a psychic. I have visions sometimes."

{140}

"Oh, I see. And your vision alarmed you?"

To tell the truth, the vision I had before bed was tame, even boring, compared with what I experienced afterward, when I was asleep. But I can't tell anyone about that dream, ever. Besides, it was just a dream. No big deal. The memory of it brings a rainstorm of tingles to my neck and arms, but I shake them away and describe the vision: "It was of you walking down our street. In crunchy leaves."

He tilts his head.

"Leaves that have fallen? Get it?" A moment passes, and finally I say, "Do leaves not fall in Otherworld?"

He shakes his head.

"Oh. Well, leaves die and fall off the trees here, before winter."

He looks alarmed. "Horrible! Why?"

"It has to do with the seasons, I think, but the trees aren't dead, they're just . . ." I stop, sigh. I do not need to be playing Bill Nye the Science Guy right now. "What I am saying is, that doesn't usually happen until the end of this month. After October fifteenth. After our birthday. So how could you be here, walking on crunchy leaves, when you are supposed to be *there*?"

A light clicks on in his attic. "Ohhhh."

"Yeah. So something must go wrong with this plan." I take a deep breath and stare hard at the ground, trying to think of what could possibly be the kink. The plan seemed so easy, so foolproof. All we had to do was make sure Cam was in the . . . Oh no. Poor Cam. "What am I going to tell Cam? I told him everything would be fine, and now . . ."

Pip digs his hands into his pockets and says, "Is it possible your vision is wrong?"

"No, no, no. My visions are never wrong. Ask anyone." So

what could go awry? Pip had agreed to go along with it, and so as long as the fairies didn't find out, we were clear. But maybe they did. Maybe they knew everything. They are such a nosy bunch of bugs. "Maybe Dawn finds out."

Of course! Of course she must have caught wind of something. That would explain everything.

In fact, maybe she already knows. Maybe she's already trying to toy with the plan. That would explain why I was having weird visions of Pip. Dawn's magic is very powerful. She is controlling my thoughts, trying to make me fall for Pip so that I will forget about Cam forever. She's getting into my dreams. Cam said that she would do anything to remove any barrier to delivering him to Otherworld.

That makes sense! I could never really have feelings for a guy like Pencil Box Pip. That would be ridiculous.

Damn fairy magic.

Pip scratches his chin. "Is it possible the current course of events could be altered, thus changing the outcome?"

"No, my visions are always right. Nothing can change it!" My voice rises in a glass-breaking crescendo. I'm trembling. "I mean, if they're going to find out anyway, there's really nothing we can do."

Pip tries to put a hand on my shoulder, but I shake it off.

"This is bad. Really bad. It's over. We might as well give up. We're done for."

Pip scratches his chin. "Interesting."

I wrap my arms around my body and stare at him, annoyed. "What do you mean, 'interesting'? How is our lives' falling apart interesting?"

He looks at the ground. "Well, you just said we should give up. So basically, you'll be guaranteeing that your vision comes true."

I scowl at him. "Well, what do you think I should do? Fight to keep him here? If I do, I'll only lose in the end. My vision confirms it."

He gives me a blank look. "Interesting."

My scowl deepens. "What?"

"In Otherworld, fairies spend years learning to control the magical powers they inherit on their sixteenth birthday. Because if they can't control them, they'll be consumed by them."

"And you're saying . . . ," I say bitterly.

"You're letting your powers control you, instead of the other way around."

I think about Cam and how he never wanted to know his future. I'd always thought he was crazy, but he did have a point. He didn't want to know if they'd win the championship last year, because he was afraid of coasting, of falling into a rut and not giving it his all. And maybe, just knowing his future, he could have changed it. Maybe, had he known, they wouldn't have won. Maybe it is better not to know.

I sigh. "So what are you saying I should do?"

"About what?"

I whirl around and come face to face with Cam. Literally. Before, it was face to pectorals. Now I could look directly into his eyes, if I weren't feeling so ashamed. Instead, I find myself studying my own flip-flops and a French pedicure that's gone to hell over the past weekend. "Um, Pip and I have a project to do for class."

Cam is fiddling with his pants, trying to pull them up. I notice he's dug an extra notch into his belt. He pulls his T-shirt over his waistband and grimaces in disgust. "For geometry?"

"Yeah," I mumble.

He inspects me. "Why do you look like you're going to hurl?"

I say something about it being a hard project and brilliantly segue with, "But enough about that! How is everything going with you?"

He shrugs. "Fine. Cool."

I look upward, toward his pink halo, and say, "What's up, Dawn?" The halo shivers a little, then quickly floats off.

"She hates that you can see her," Cam whispers.

I mutter, "It's not my fault that her spell is defective."

"Seriously, play nice."

"Whatever. Listen, about what we talked about . . . ," I begin, ready to open up about my vision. Yes, he needs to know if the plan will fail. He needs to know that, despite our best efforts, we won't be together. But then I look him in the eyes, and they're bright and hopeful and full of love for me.

"What's up?" he says, casually. Relaxed. More like the old Cam.

No. I can't let him down. I won't be the one to let his hopes come crashing down. Not today.

"No worries," I finally say, forcing a grin.

"No worries," he says, smiling the first real smile I've seen in days.

Pip's eyes are boring into me, and right before Cam slides his arm around my shoulders and pulls me toward the school, I see him mouth the words "Don't give up."

That's the worst. Now Cam's depending on me to save him from Otherworld, when everything inside me is telling me it's impossible.

I SLINK INTO geometry class and slide into my chair, miserable. Here I was, getting my hopes up—getting Cam's hopes up—that it really was possible to save him from Otherworld, and now I know it can't happen. And yes, maybe Pip does have a point. Maybe I shouldn't be letting my visions control my actions. It would help if some of my visions were a little off from time to time. But I've predicted hundreds of futures, and I've never been wrong. Not once.

Sometimes this gift really gets on my nerves.

Eden is giggling at me. For no reason. She's unusually peppy today, which is dangerous, because I'm unusually on the verge of throwing punches at anything that gets in my way. She tosses her hair like she's in a shampoo commercial, then throws her arm over the back of the chair and gives me an openmouthed grin.

"What?" I snap.

I didn't think it was possible, but the grin gets wider. I can almost see her tonsils. "Notice anything different?"

I so do not want to be playing guessing games right now. "You got permanent eyeliner?" I venture halfheartedly.

"Ew, you know I would never do that." She tosses her hair again, so that a couple of reddish strands land on my desk. Eden sheds worse than a Labrador.

"Sara had an aneurysm and they want you to fill in as head cheerleader?"

She giggles way too much in response to my lame joke and says, "I wish." Then she pulls her hair back into a ponytail and lets it fall down her back.

How annoying. I'm three seconds away from whipping out a pair of scissors and going snip crazy. "What is wrong with your hair? You—"

But that's when I see it. A reddish blotch, right on the side of her neck. It's horrifyingly big and shaped kind of like Texas. She winks at me, like a little sexpot, so *not* like the old lady I'd envisioned sitting at home talking to her Precious Moments figurines.

"It's a hickey!" she cries out, loud enough for half the class to swing their heads in our direction.

"Pretty." I sigh. So, just perfect. While the rest of the sophomore class had a carefree weekend filled with youthful debauchery, I was trying to salvage the remains of my pathetic fairy relationship. I'm sure they partied like it was 1999 while I was off dancing the tango with Dorky Dorkison.

Eden dips her head under the clouds for a second to notice the bandage on my arm. "Oh, my God! What happened there?"

"I . . . fell," I mutter.

"Is it broken?"

"Just black-and-blue."

"Oh, my God!" she repeats. "You poor thing. It's like this weekend, the whole earth shifted or something."

I stare at her blankly.

"I mean, you're injured." She waves her hand toward the front of the room, where Pip is still rifling through his pencil case. In all the weekend's hysteria, I'd forgotten to steal and burn it. "Geekboy is hot." She juts her finger toward the purple bruise mingling with her freckles, and the mondo-grin returns. "And *this* awesome thing."

"You think he's hot?" I ask, watching Pip as he chews nervously on his pinky fingernail. Though bloody nail stubs aren't exactly attractive, he still looks a bit scrumptious. I wonder how much of that is due to my powers of makeover and how much is due to Dawn's spell.

She shrugs. "Sure. Kind of."

Only then do I realize I am staring at him, jaw dropped, a pool of drool ready to spill over my bottom lip. I close my mouth quickly and say, "So, who?"

Her eyes narrow. "Huh?"

"Who's the vampire?"

She's still squinting like Clint Eastwood.

It obviously isn't getting through, so I point to the disgusting bruise and say, "Who. Did. That?"

She rolls her eyes. "Duh. Mike."

Now it's my turn. "Mike who?"

"Duh!" she says again. "Kensington. Who else?"

"He didn't."

"He did!" she squeals.

"Hell he did. He's gay!" I burst out, and realize a quarter of a second too late that I probably should have whispered that part, since everyone is now staring at us again. "Or, at least, I thought he was," I say, more softly this time.

She glares at me. "God. The people in this school really get on my nerves sometimes. Can't a guy dress well and still be hetero?"

"Well, yeah, but—"

She shrugs and points at the hickey. "Everyone can be wrong. It's called groupthink." She says this last part very condescendingly.

I stare at her, unbelieving. "So, wait. You *knew* everyone thought he was gay? And you still went after him?"

She nods.

"My intuition is usually right about things like this," I murmur. "Maybe he's just confused."

"Ri-ight." She giggles. "Maybe you're the one who is confused."

Pip turns around and grins at me, still sucking on a fingernail. And I find myself breathless, shivering, wondering what it would be like if he really did touch me like he did in my dream. And then I think of Cam and want to stab myself with my pen.

Eden is right. I am definitely confused.

30

THROUGHOUT THE PERIOD, Pip keeps looking back at me and mouthing, "Don't give up," so much so that by the time Tanner throws out a pop quiz, I've lost all concentration. I miss half the questions, which just about seals the deal of me never reaching teacher's pet status in his heart in my lifetime. Though I'm used to teachers beaming at me, when the period ends and Tanner scowls as he collects my paper, I can't bring myself to care.

If I was wrong about Mike, maybe that vision of Pip is wrong, too?

In the hallway, I see Eden already engaged in a massive PDA with Mike at the next classroom over. Even when she's on her tiptoes, he's, like, two feet taller, and as he brings her face up to his, he gets this rabid, desirous gleam in his eyes, like he might swallow her head. So, he is enjoying it. People passing by are doing double takes, just as confused as I am. Mike Kensington. Gay Mike. Who'd've thunk?

Okay, so I'd never actually envisioned Mike playing for the other team. My intuition has always been just as brilliant as my psychic ability, which makes sense. And ever since I met Mike, my intuition has screamed, "Gay!" So for me to be that off-base is . . . well, is something that has never happened before.

As Mike drapes himself over her, it makes me think of Cam. The way Cam once was. Biting my lip, I turn away, ready to barrel down whoever is in my way, in search of the nearest girls' room. But I'm stopped dead in my tracks by Pip's goofy grin.

"People are too damn happy today," I mutter, pushing past him to stop myself from acting on the instinct to reach out and touch him.

"I got you something," he says, shuffling to catch up to me. "For helping me this weekend."

Stay away from him, a little voice in the part of my head that's not being controlled by Dawn screams. *Be tough. Avoid all urges to stick your tongue down his throat, as they are just the product of fairy magic.*

"I don't need anything," I say, noticing for the first time that he's holding a small plastic bag.

He hands me the bag and I peek inside. It's a tube of Wet n Wild lipstick. In hideous Day-Glo orange. "All the females at the drugstore were purchasing them."

I raise an eyebrow at him, highly doubtful. "In this color?"

"It's beautiful, isn't it? Reminds me of the sunset in Otherworld."

I close the bag and tuck it into my purse. Though I'm

actively trying to be cold to him, I can't help being touched by the gesture. "Thank you. Really. It must be very beautiful there."

He nods. "That is what I miss about it the most, I think. The sunset."

That's what I need to hear right now—how much he misses Otherworld and can't wait to return. "So you really don't mind going back?"

His face brightens. "You mean you're not giving up?"

"My vision could be a little off," I admit, watching Mike gnaw on Eden's earlobe. "And I can't. Not with Cam depending on me."

"You'll see, everything will work out."

I don't want to think about it anymore. I quickly change the subject. "Have you asked anyone yet?"

He gives me a sheepish grin. "I didn't think there was much of a reason to, since I will be going back to Otherworld."

I start to put a reassuring hand on his back but stop halfway, deciding that would be a mistake. Besides, I'd had enough physical contact with him last night. "Of course there is! There's nothing saying your last night in this world can't be a little fun. You should just enjoy yourself."

"All right. But . . ."

"Don't be nervous. Trust me, you're a hottie, and any girl would be happy to go with you. Remember: confidence."

"Confidence," he repeats, surveying the market expressionlessly, as if watching cars pass on a highway.

"See, lots to choose from," I tell him, more assured in the thought that whomever he takes to our party will not be leaving with him. Once dear, sweet Pip is safely in Otherworld, we can give the poor girl a ride back from the city and tell her that he ran away to join the circus or something. "Did you have anyone in mind?"

"Um." He digs his hands in his pockets. "I thought I would just ask one of the ones who asked me this morning."

The hallway's awfully noisy, so maybe I didn't hear him right. But I could have sworn he said someone already asked him. Scratch that; he said "one of the ones," meaning that *more than one person* already asked him. Which, considering it's only nine on Monday morning, is impossible. Isn't it? "Wait. What? Who already asked you?"

His standard deer-in-headlights look returns. "I don't know their names. There was a girl with very long yellow hair, almost white. And she had very nice teeth."

I wave my hand in front of him and he stops talking right away. This is bad. Obviously. This is the thing that spells doom for our plan. I had no idea that Pip could work this quickly. I mean, sometimes my powers of makeover scare me even more than my psychic abilities. Or perhaps Dawn is using her magic to make Pip irresistible to every girl on the planet so that I become jealous and fall even harder for him. Either way, one thing is clear. Pip is definitely a loose cannon.

And I should have known by the way Gizelle, the events manager at the Toad, fell over Pip that multiple girls at school would do the same thing. If Pip could hook a date for the party this quickly . . . who knows, by Friday he could be engaged! And Pip, who has never known love before, might become so infatuated with his date that when the time comes, he'll refuse to go to Otherworld. Pip seems trustworthy, but he has no idea how crazy love can make a person. And people do all sorts of nutty things for love.

Just look at me. I'm steering myself right into the mental-breakdown lane.

"Look," I tell him, "maybe you're right. You should just go to this thing alone."

He bites his lip. "If you say so."

"Unless you don't want to. You can take someone, as long as you . . ."

He stops me then by putting his hands squarely on my arms. His hands are big, powerful, and feel warm on my bare shoulders. I blink away flashes of last night's dream, his skin against mine. When he looks into my eyes, I feel a little weak. Dizzy. Definitely not like myself. His words are spoken with a calm, confident voice, one I've never heard from him before. "Morgan. I will go to Otherworld on Friday night. That is my promise."

My voice fails me. Finally, I squeak out, "Okay."

He gives me a fabulous grin, with just a trace of cockiness, the essence of what has gotten him turning the head of every girl in school. Because my heart beats in double time. "You sure?"

I nod. "So you think the plan is going to work?"

His voice has more resolve and strength than I thought it was capable of. "I know it will."

Just then, there's a squeal, and a gaggle of girls comes stampeding from the direction of the guidance office. As it gets closer, I see a flash of hideous color and realize that it's headed by Sierra Martin, wearing a god-awful lime green pipe-cleaner thing in her hair and the third Monday-morning destined-for-the-nuthouse grin I've seen today. Her face is red from bounding down the hall, so she looks a little like a drunk leprechaun. She catches a glimpse of me and sneers, and before I can say anything, she holds out a very official-looking burgundy envelope.

Oh. Now I get it.

"Harvard?" I ask.

She nods smugly and continues down the hall, her followers at her heels.

"Congrats," I call after her.

When I catch my breath, Pip is still watching me. "So, you see, you shouldn't let your visions dictate how you live your life," he is saying.

And for the first time, I believe that he is right.

31

WALKING THE TIGHTROPE without a net can actually be a good thing. Sure, anything can happen, bad or good, but it beats believing Cam and I are doomed and not being able to do anything about it.

It's been a while since I've been able to think about the party without thinking of it as Cam's last night in this world. So at the end of the day, when I'm approached by a couple of freshmen looking for last-minute invites to my party, I don't mind handing them out. I even chat them up, promise to tell their futures sometime, forget about the fairies for a while, which is something I haven't done in days. It feels good to think about something in the present, for once, instead of constantly obsessing about the future.

By the time I'm done handing out invites, the hallways are clear and all the buses have left the front of the building. I can hear a couple of stray notes from a trumpet and a saxophone as the marching band warms up on the field out back, so I know it's late. Cam is probably at practice. Maybe I'll just go home, kick up, and spend time with the only man in my life that, for once, *isn't* driving me crazy right now: my dad. For the first time in ages, I don't think I'd mind relaxing on the couch with him, letting him explain *General Hospital* to me.

I put my books in my locker and slam the door. When I turn around, I jump back. Cam is there, leaning against the row of lockers across the hall, expressionless, arms folded. His red-rimmed eyes say it all.

"What happened?" I ask when I've finally gotten over the shock. "Why aren't you at practice?"

He straightens up and walks across the hall to me, and I gasp. In the past few hours, he must have shrunk five more inches. I can see clearly over the top of his head. Meaning, I'm *taller* than he is. He's wearing a baggy sweatshirt, but it's pulling away from his shoulders as if he were wearing a back-pack under his clothes. His jeans are cuffed but they still drag on the ground, completely covering all but the toes of his shoes.

"You know why," he says, in a voice I don't recognize. It's higher-pitched, twangy, like a country singer's. And lacking all the confidence it once held. I guess this doesn't surprise me; nothing about him is the same anymore.

"You can't play?"

He shakes his head, his shoulders drooping forward. "Our first game is Thursday, and I can barely throw the ball ten feet."

"But can't they see something is going on with you? You're a foot shorter than you were on Friday."

"I'm not sure they can. I don't think anyone can. Except you."

"Me? Why just me?"

He shrugs. "Maybe for the same reason you can see Dawn. Maybe because you know me better than anyone. Anyway, they're focused on the win. And I'm letting them down. They're pissed."

"Have you told Scab? He would understand."

"He's the worst of them. And what am I supposed to tell him? I can't play because I'm a fairy?" He shakes the thought away. "He would laugh his ass off at me. They all would."

"So what did you tell them?"

"I just walked off. I told them I was quitting and to use their second string."

"Second string? That's Tommy Miller, and he sucks."

"At this point, he's better than me. Anyone is." He rakes his hands through his black hair, and I catch a glimpse of a nub of skin poking out from over his ears. He catches my stunned expression and lifts a lock of his hair up so that I can get a better look. "Yeah, they're pointy. Hot, huh?"

"They're kind of cute," I say, really meaning it. "Don't get down. Look, the plan is going to work. We'll be together."

"And I'll be a freak."

"You just said nobody can see the changes in you except me. So what does it matter? I will love you no matter what. You know that. This is great."

His face is dark, darker than I've ever seen it. In the past few days, he's been spiraling downward, and nothing I've told him has helped. "I don't know if I can do this," he says, his new, strange voice nearly cracking.

"You can," I tell him. "Cam Browne can do anything, remember?"

"That was the old one," he says, exhaling slowly. "Not this one."

"Okay, so you may not be able to throw a football anymore. But big deal. There are other things in life. Just move on to the next thing."

"But what is my next thing?" His voice is louder now, and there is frustration in it. "I played football because it came naturally to me. My body was good for it. Do you know what my body is good for now?"

"It's good for a lot of—"

"Only one thing. Fairying."

I flash back to the vision of Pip walking, his feet crunching, on the brown leaves and catch my heart before it forces its way out of my throat. I thought I'd convinced him to stay, and over the past couple of days, he'd seemed more resolute in going through with the plan. And now this. I'd thought I'd imagined every possible situation that could force our plan to fail, but not this. I never thought *he* would be the reason the plan wouldn't work. "So, you're giving in. You want to leave me."

He won't look into my eyes, so I already know the answer. "I don't think I have a choice."

I know people say that in critical times, their entire life flashes in front of their eyes. At that second, snippets of our relationship gallop through my mind—playing Game Boy with him on his hospital bed for hours on end when he was sick with asthma; watching him throw back an entire carton of milk and package of Oreos every day after school; my fifth-birthday party, where we accidentally both gave each other a Sit 'n Spin; and last Christmas, when he got me an opal ring—my

{158}

birthstone. The fairies have obviously clouded his mind, because he can't possibly be thinking straight if he wants all of that to come to an end. I drop my bag and walk over to him, put my arms around his neck. His body feels small, weak, like it could crack apart. "You'll be miserable there."

"I know. I'll be miserable here, so what's the difference?"

"Me," I blurt out. "At least here, you'll have me."

He nods, a gleam returning to his eye. "You're right. I'm letting the guys get to me. Football's not the only thing in life."

"Right."

"There's loads of things I can do besides playing football." He stops, picks up my bag, and hefts it up onto his shoulder, and for the first time, he has a bit of trouble with the weight. Then, his tortured voice sighs, "I just have to figure out what they are."

32

THAT NIGHT, THE weather is beautiful, so I spend it on our front porch, surrounded by old copies of my mother's magazines, drinking cinnamon tea and looking up every so often to see if Cam is around. But his house is completely dark. As usual, he's in training. When I left him this afternoon, he'd mentioned something about having a first assignment. He was—no surprise—dreading it.

I guess that's why I am on a mission, going through cheesy, feel-good articles from this supermarket checkout-aisle rag. I'd remembered seeing a news story on television a long time ago about a soldier who lost half his head in Iraq. He couldn't do many things, but he discovered a passion for working with kids. I remember him telling the camera, "When I had my accident, I didn't think life was worth living. But now, my life is so much more fulfilling than I ever imagined." I got to thinking, maybe that's what Cam needs. A little boost so that he can see that his life isn't over. So I'm finding stories about people who faced adversity and triumphed, putting them into a collage, with hopes it might lift his spirits.

Like my mom's *sfogliatelle,* it's a long shot, but what kind of girlfriend would I be if I didn't try?

I flick a tiny insect off my forearm just as a voice calls from the darkness beyond the porch. "Hey, there!" At first I think it's Cam, but the lifeless boy I saw this afternoon wouldn't have that energy in his voice. It's only a second before Pip launches himself over a hedge and plants himself on the glider, next to me. "What are you doing?"

He's sitting just inches from me, and I can see golden stubble on his chin. The look definitely works. Why is it that a week ago, he was nothing but a baby-faced little boy, and now he's . . .

Oh, right. Fairy magic.

"You're happy," I say, trying to avoid looking into his eyes. How can I be so happy to see him and so anxious to have him leave at the same time?

He swallows back his grin. "Sorry. Are things not good with Cameron?"

"He's depressed. I'm cutting out inspirational stories to cheer him up."

"That's a nice idea," he says, grabbing a magazine from the stack. "I will help."

He flips to a page, begins to read, and suddenly starts to pant, turning red. Shaking. I think he may be having convulsions. "What?" I ask.

He has tears streaming from his eyes. "Listen to this," he says, reading from the magazine. "'Two fish swim into a wall. One says to the other, "Dam!"'"

I am not sure if he is laughing or dying. He pounds the arm of the glider with his fist and fights to breathe. All I can do is stare. Dawn has to be using her magic to make him irresistible to the opposite sex; it is not physically possible for a guy to be that lame and still be a girl magnet. "Amusing," I say. "But not exactly inspirational."

"Sorry." He quickly quiets and starts to flip the pages. I try to go back to my own magazine, but I can't help peeking at him every so often. Even without the makeover, he's an interesting guy. He has a look of pure concentration on his face—lips pursed, eyes focused—as if he really wants to help with this project. It's sweet, the way he is, so untouched by everything bad in this world, so naïve and trusting. I can't believe I'd even thought for a second that he'd fall in love and ruin the plan. Of course he would never go back on his word. He's like a child, and with children, promises are pinky sworn, solemn, and unbreakable. They mean something.

After a while, he looks up at me, triumphant. "I found one. This guy lost both his arms in a motorcycle accident but still runs marathons."

Up until that moment, I hadn't realized I was staring at him, openmouthed, in a dream state. I snap back to reality and finally choke out, "Um. Yeah. Great. Thanks."

I pass him the scissors, and he begins to clip out the article. Every so often, he stops and screws up his face. "I am wondering if there is anything else I can do for him," he says thoughtfully.

Of course he is. Saint Pip. "You're doing enough. Seriously. I don't know if I thanked you for helping to keep us together . . . but thank you."

"You and Cam have been very good to me, even when others were not. So I am happy to return the favor," he says.

At that moment, something hits me. "But you are human. You are capable of love. And if you go to Otherworld . . ."

He plays with the sleeve of his shirt. "Honestly, Morgan. I have given it thought, and I'm not interested in that."

"You aren't? How do you know?"

"There seems to be quite a lot of pain involved."

"I can't deny that. Sometimes I think I'd be better off without it." I motion toward the magazines and grin. "Sometimes it's a real pain in the ass."

He shrugs. "Of course, the way I see it, you're both better people because of it. Right?"

I think for a moment. "Me, definitely. Him? I don't know. I guess."

He slides the article into my pile. "Is that what you think?"

"Well, yeah. Look at Cam. I mean, he's amazing. Everything he touches turns to gold. You said that Cam thought I was brave. That's only because of him. In this world, I'm just . . . Cam's Girlfriend. Or Free Psychic Reading Girl. I doubt half the people who are coming to our party on Friday even know my name."

He looks back at the magazine and sighs. "I told you Cam was a changeling. Do you know what a changeling is?"

I think for a moment, back to when Pip gave me the mind-blowing rundown on all things fey. "You said he was sick."

"Right. From the very beginning his brother, Azizl, was the stronger of the two sons. Massif and the royal court assumed Azizl would eventually be king and Cameron would wither and die. So they cast him out of Otherworld. They never expected him to live to reach his sixteenth birthday."

"But he didn't die."

Pip nods. "But he was supposed to. Why didn't he?"

"I remember, he had asthma. He was in the hospital at least once a month. It was a horrible thing for a little kid to have to go through. I remember visiting him all the time. I'd make him cards, and—" He's nodding at me as if he knows all this. I finally say, "Are you saying he didn't die because of me?"

He shrugs. "I think you had a lot to do with it."

"Really?" I let that sink in for a moment. It seems so ridiculous that playing a few games of Tetris with Cam could make him well. "Even if that *is* true, instead of thanking me, Massive Jerk wants to take him from me."

"His name is Massif. But yes."

I blow a strand of hair out of my eyes. "At the mall, we have a saying for that. 'No refunds, no exchanges.' Tough luck."

"I know it isn't fair," he whispers. "And maybe if Azizl hadn't died, Massif wouldn't care so much. But Cameron is now the only heir to Otherworld's throne."

"Cam would make a great king," I admit. But only if I could be his queen.

He checks his watch. "I must go. Will you be all right?"

I nod, feeling a twinge of sadness that he can't stay, but happy that he's looking out for me. Maybe it was Cam who told him to, but something tells me that he would have done it anyway. "Where are you going?"

"I'm courting a girl from our class. Like you told me to."

My stomach flip-flops. "Courting? Oh really?" I force a smile. "Which girl?"

He stands up, shakes down the legs of his jeans. "Sara Phillips."

I bite my tongue so hard, I can taste the blood. Sara Phillips,

{164}

ethereal head cheerleader. The word "perfect" constantly swirls around her head, along with furry cartoon animals and singing birds. Scab has had a crush on her since our last finger-painting class, and I don't think she's dated anyone in our school, ever. In fact, the only guys she dates are college ones, frat boys with Beamers and Sigma Chi Whatever sweatshirts. They come to the games in droves to drool over her matchstick legs in that cute little skirt.

"She—is she one of the girls who asked you to the party?" I spit out, the words tumbling over one another in an incomprehensible heap.

He nods.

So let me get this straight. Sara asked him? The untouchable Sara Phillips likes Pip?

Okay, some fairy magic is definitely at play here. There is no other explanation. My face must be frozen in horror, because he says, "Why? Is she bad?"

"Um, no. Not exactly. Just don't—" My mouth hangs open, contemplating how to finish. *"Don't give in and kiss her when she looks at you with those pathetic doe eyes of hers"? "Don't fall for her"? "Don't be the utterly perfect, sweet guy you've been all this time so that she falls for you"?* After all, he's just "courting." He's just doing exactly what I told him to do. And why shouldn't he? In another few days he'll be returning to Otherworld, where falling in love isn't possible. I should be encouraging him to have as much fun in this world as he can. Finally, I swallow and say, "Just have fun."

"Sure. Have a good night, Morgan," he says, hopping down the porch steps, taking all three at once. And he disappears into the darkness, leaving me with a pile of magazines . . . a pile of inspiration. And yet, why do I feel so uninspired?

33

ON TUESDAY MORNING, something happens that has never before occurred in my life on this earth. When I come downstairs, my mother is not standing at the door to the kitchen, carton of Tropicana in hand. In fact, the house is completely devoid of any breakfasty smells—no eggs, no bacon, none of the elaborate morning meals my mother usually cooks and I rarely have time to eat. Our Mr. Coffee isn't even brewing. Not that I was hungry, but I assumed this day would come only when my mother was dead and buried. So naturally that worries me.

I'm trying to close the front door while simultaneously holding a Pop-Tart between my teeth and stuffing my geometry book into my backpack, when I see her. She's sitting on the front steps in her typical morning attire of housecoat and slippers, a full trash basket between her feet. She looks dazed.

"Need help with that?" I ask.

She shakes her head. "Hi, hon. No, I already took care of it."

I peer into the container. "It's full. Don't you want it at the curb?"

She blinks as if waking from a dream. "Oh yes. I just . . ."

"Are you okay?"

"Yes. But the most amazing thing has happened," she says, her voice sounding anything but fine. It sounds faraway, lacking in energy.

I have to pry the trash can from her fingers. She doesn't seem to realize she's holding it in a white-knuckled death grip. "What?"

The same soft voice floats up, barely audible. "Mrs. Nelson is bringing Gracie home today."

It's sad; the little ranch across the street has been dark all week. I look past the bushes, toward the blackened windows, and say, "To make her more comfortable in her last days?"

She closes her eyes. "She's fine."

I stand there for a moment, not comprehending. "What do you mean by 'fine'?"

"Mrs. Nelson said that not only is the cancer gone, but the doctors say it was like it never existed in the first place. It's completely gone."

"But . . . two days ago she only had a week to live, tops."

"I know. It's a miracle."

"Your *sfogliatelle?*"

She looks at me and nods. "What other explanation could there be?"

{167}

"Sweet. Well, I'm glad she's okay."

"I think I should go into business with that recipe," she says, struggling to get to her feet. Looking out across the lawn, she says, "Well, there's another person who is back from the dead. I haven't seen Cam in ages."

I whirl around and catch Cam waiting at the line between our houses. Grinning big. Since that's the first glorious grin I've seen in a while, it's obvious he got the collage of stories I'd made for him last night. After midnight, I'd gone over and left it poking out of his mailbox so that he'd see it first thing in the morning.

"He looks well fed and healthy, as usual," she says to me, poking her head around the ivy trellis to get a better look at him.

I shake my head in bewilderment. So, it's true. I'm the only one who can see the ears, the wings, the tiny stature that Cam now has. I'm the only one who notices the cloud of pink swirling around his head. Even my mother, who can detect a fleck of dust the second it falls to our carpet, can't see it.

"Well, tell him we miss him around here. Invite him to dinner tonight. *Pasta e fagioli.* His favorite."

"Everything you make is his favorite," I answer. His smile, from across the lawn, feels like sunlight after a long rain. "But I think he's busy."

"Shame. Well, one day next week."

I wave goodbye, thinking that if all goes right, one day next week could be a possibility.

As I near him, Cam, my king of the fairy world, looks better and better. He looks rested, more like the old Cam, despite the fact that he's lost another few inches. I can see straight over his head.

"Hey, Boo! One, two, three," he says with a chuckle, grabbing my hand and pulling me to him.

I find myself hunching over to give him a kiss, and when he pulls me to him, it's awkward, like sitting in a small, spindly, uncomfortable chair that's in danger of breaking under my weight. But I don't care. He's smiling.

"Same to you. What's gotten you so happy?" I ask, pretending I don't know.

"My mail-order bride is passing through customs as we speak," he says, holding my hand in his. "It's a good day."

I punch him playfully, not as hard as I normally would, because I'm afraid he'll fall over. He's right; the whole world seems brighter. Now I wonder why I was tinged with concern at Pip having a date with Sara. All of that seems so unimportant right now. "Isn't Pip coming with us?" I ask after we take a few steps toward school.

"No. I haven't seen him since yesterday."

"What do you mean?" I ask, feeling my temperature rise. "You mean he didn't get back from his date last night?"

He shrugs. "I have no idea. I was out late, too."

Panic sets in. "I mean, I hope he's okay. Our plan depends on it," I explain, taking a few cleansing breaths.

"He's fine," Cam says.

"How do you know?"

"I told you, fairies have a heightened sense of everything around them. For instance, I know you're wearing the red heart thong."

I pull away and wrap my arms around me. "What?"

"Are you?"

I bite my lip. I can't remember.

He laughs. "I have no idea. It was just a guess. But you should see your face."

Blah. Guys may be immature, but guy fairies give the word a whole new meaning.

He wraps an arm around me and squeezes. I remember when his squeezes would rearrange my internal organs, but this one is so light, I barely feel it. He says something reassuring and nuzzles my ear so that it tickles and I have to swat him away. And that's when I look up at Cam's house, onto the porch, and see it.

The collage I made. The orange construction-paper cover is poking out from the top of the mailbox, just as I had left it.

I turn to him, confused.

And he's happy . . . why?

34

THE MYSTERY DOESN'T become any clearer by the time we get to school. Cam won't tell me why he has that grin plastered on his face. I venture that maybe he got his throwing arm back, or that perhaps Dawn has laid off being such the drill sergeant, but he just shakes his head and says, "It's part of the fairy code. Confidential," which makes me hate the fairy world even more.

"What? What? Tell me!" I whine, knowing that he can't take my pathetic preschooler routine for more than a few minutes.

He runs his fingers up and down my back, leans toward me so that our foreheads are touching, and says, "Remember how we talked about moving on to the next thing?"

I nod. "What? Have you found your next thing?"

But he just grins again and refuses to say more. Grr.

When we part, I head down to the music wing, toward my locker. That's when I hear the yelling. People tear down the hall, past me. "Come on!" a shaggy-haired guy in a Beastie Boys T-shirt yells to his friend, and then I hear a snippet of what sounds like "kicking ass" and I know it's a fight. Few things can bring the otherwise comatose student body at Stevens to life like a good brawl, but they've never interested me. I walk at a leisurely pace, just hoping there's no blood on or surrounding my locker, when I hear another person shout. I can just make out "In the gym" and "That new kid."

New kid.

Pip.

I forget about making it to my locker, about the wrath of Tanner. I find myself at the doorway to the gym, out of breath, though I can't remember running there. There, in the center of the room, is a rabid swarm of at least fifty students, all chanting in rhythm, "Go! Go!"

I'm elbowed and punched a dozen times before I finally make it to the center and see exactly what I'd feared.

There's a motionless body on the ground, in fetal position, and Scab is on top of it, his full weight bearing into it, pummeling it with both his fists like a jackhammer. I know the body is Pip's; Pip might have the strength to hit back, and even to win against a guy like Scab, but he never would. I wish for a second that Cam could be here, to talk some sense into his best friend, but I know he's on the other side of the building. And so it's all a blur when I force my way into the center of the circle and scream for Scab to stop.

My cry doesn't break through his delirium. Instead of

obeying, he starts to kick Pip in the stomach, and Pip's body lurches inches across the hardwood with every motion.

Cam would kill Scab if he laid a hand on me, so I feel safe going in there, despite how crazed the guy looks. With my good hand, I try to pull back on his arm, but I'm shocked when he throws his shoulder back, lashing me in the face. The thunder of the jeering crowd and the beating of my heart are muffled in my ears as I slide down to the hard surface of the gymnasium floor. I feel for my nose, which is beginning to ache numbly, and when I bring my fingers in front of my eyes, they are coated in red.

He is *so* going to get it when Cam hears about this.

And still, Scab doesn't stop. The crowd grows louder. The size and volume seem to increase along with the drama, so the sight of my blood forming neat, round droplets on the shiny wood floor has launched them into a frenzy. Wiping my face with the back of my hand, I somehow get the nerve to throw myself behind Pip, and drag him a few feet away. "What the hell?" is all I can bark out.

Scab looks up, a bit of humanness returning to his face, and for the first time seems shocked to see me bleeding.

"Is this because of Sara?" I yell at him, then pull Pip back and look at his face. He has a bloody lip, probably from the first sucker punch Scab threw at him, but other than that, I think I took worse. He stirs and makes it to his elbows, a "What happened?" look on his face.

Scab looks down at him in disgust. "It's because he's a loser."

"How do you know that?" I ask, my voice trembling, though I concentrate on every word to keep it even.

Scab shakes his head. "Obvious. He can't even fight."

Pip is rubbing his tender jaw. I help him to his feet and see

John Vaughn standing there, in his football jersey, holding a football. "John," I say, pointing out across the gym. "Go long."

John looks at me blankly, and I have to pry the football from him with my bloody hands. "You heard me. Go!"

He shrugs and heads out across the gym until he's nearly half a field's length away. The crowd watches—as does Scab, with a half-tired, half-still-dying-to-pummel-Pip look on his face.

I hand Pip the ball and nod at him.

He barely has to put in any effort. Despite the fact that he's crumpled and woozy, he returns my nod, pulls the ball back behind his ear, and robotically lets go. It sails perfectly into John's hands, as if he were pulling it to him with a magnet.

"'Obvious,' huh. Was that?" I ask Scab.

Scab doesn't answer, just stands there like the rest of the crowd. Mouth open, completely silent.

35

WHEN THE TEACHERS arrive, the mob quickly disperses. A faculty member ushers Scab toward the principal's office, and in the midst of all the commotion, I'm able to walk Pip to an alcove behind the bleachers, to help him catch his breath. He looks at me gratefully, but there is a hollow, distant glaze in his eyes.

I take the last remaining tissue from my bag, divide it, and offer one part to him. Then I dab the other half cautiously over my nose. "He's a jerk. He's had a crush on Sara forever. I should have warned you, but I didn't know he'd—"

"That's all right." He is staring at the slats of the bleachers ahead of him, or at nothing. His voice is soft but very even.

"I guess you can't get back to Otherworld soon enough now, right?" I say, more lightly.

A slow, sad smile dawns on his face. He turns to look at me, then grimaces, clenching his side.

"What?" I ask him. "It hurts?"

"Not so bad. I was just thinking."

"About?"

"About you. You don't think you're brave, and yet . . ."

"Listen, it's no big deal. I've known Scab forever. The only thing scary about him is the way he shovels food into his mouth." I look down at his shirt, which is scuffed with black marks near his ribs, where Scab had kicked him. "Oh, God. Do you think something is broken? Lift up your shirt. Let me see."

"I'm fine." He takes a step back, pulls his shirt down over his waist, very modestly.

"Come on, don't be shy; let me see," I say, reaching for it. He tries to push my hand away but finally stops. I pull the fabric up, just to midchest, and see those abs I'd seen last Friday, this time close-up. They really are every bit as glorious as I'd remembered. They're smattered with a few purplish marks, but nothing too horrible. And soon, I'm touching them, running my fingers along his ribs, saying, "Does this hurt? How about this?" and trying not to think of what I am doing in anything more than a medical sense. He's breathing so heavily, I feel it hot on my forehead, and I can almost hear his heartbeat.

"I guess I'm going to live," he murmurs, ending with a quick laugh, and I realize it's the first time he ever attempted humor with me. So, he's learning. Maybe last night's fabulous date with Sara unleashed that in him.

"Turn around—let me check your back," I say, trying to force him to whirl about, but he stands there, feet planted. He's trying to pull down his shirt, but if he wouldn't throw punches at Scab, he's definitely not going to put up resistance with me. I easily twist him to the side and wrangle up his battered Gap tee, and that's when I see them.

Scars. Red slashes, crisscrossing his lower back. And probably farther up, but his shirt is covering his shoulder blades. Now they're just hard tracks, the skin shiny and thick around the edges, but when they were new, the pain must have been unbearable. Worse than anything I've felt in my lifetime.

"What are those?"

He skirts away from me and covers himself, clearly humiliated. "It's nothing. I'm fine."

"Pip, that doesn't look fine. That looks horrible. What is that from? Did that happen to you in Otherworld?"

He looks away, then tries to walk past me. "I have to get to class."

I put my hand on his chest. "Not yet. Is this what they do to humans in Otherworld?"

"No." He seems adamant. "Well, not all of us."

"So they did do this to you? Why?"

He sighs, wipes his eyes with the back of his hand. It's a moment before he says, "All right. I lied to you."

My heart catches in my throat. "About what?"

"About being in love."

"You said you didn't know if you were capable of that."

"I'm not sure I am now. Because I was in love, once. In Otherworld."

"Oh," I say, wondering how being in love could have gotten him a dozen red welts. I remember the conversation I'd had with him last night. He'd said before that he wasn't interested in love, because it was too painful. Yes, love can hurt, but this is a little crazy. "Was she a fairy?"

He nods. "Perhaps it was more like infatuation than love. I guess you could say I wanted so desperately to fit in with her kind.

"I promised I would do anything for her. So when she accidentally killed another fairy, I took the punishment. I was already an outcast for being human, so I assumed it would be easier for me, and she was so fragile. I was incarcerated for two of your years. It wasn't a pleasant experience."

"They hurt you in prison?"

"That wasn't so bad. But when I was released, nearly every fairy who did speak to me before never spoke to me again. Including her." He clenches his fists. "That was the worst part."

By the time he's done explaining, his eyes are wet, which makes me feel guilty, wonder why I'd bothered to press him to tell the story.

"As I've told you, fairies are not capable of love. She wasn't. It's not her fault. It's mine for thinking I could change her."

"That's horrible," I say, looking down at the ground to stop the tears from flowing. And the worst thing of all is that he's going to be headed back there in only three days' time. Why would any person in their right mind want to head straight back into the fire like that? Could he actually be that insane?

"You left Otherworld willingly. You don't want to go back," I say, my voice soft. "The only reason you're going back is . . . because of the plan? Because of what I asked of you?"

"It's because I know what it's like to lose someone you love."

"But if you go back, it will be even worse than before you left."

He points to his swollen jaw, dark purple in the shadows. "I'm not much better off here."

"But you can be," I tell him, unable to stop the words from coming out of my mouth. "Don't you think you'd have a better chance here? With other humans?"

And, under that logic, maybe Cam will have a better chance of fitting in with other fairies. But I refuse to think about anything logical right now.

"I can't let you . . . We can't go through with this. I will hate myself forever if I let that happen to you."

"Don't you want to be with Cam?"

I sigh. "More than anything."

"There's your answer." He smiles at me, reassuringly. "Don't worry about me. I will be fine."

Somehow, I don't believe him. I say, "Is there a way we can keep you both here?"

"No. That would upset the balance between the two worlds," he says quickly. "But, Morgan, I am fully prepared to do this for you . . ."

". . . for true love," I complete his sentence.

"Right. Because when two people love each other, nothing should stand in their way."

I mumble a thank-you. My cheeks feel hot, and I have to look away from his intense gaze. I find myself wishing he weren't such a sweetheart. Maybe that would make this feeling stop—this feeling like there's a giant seam in my middle, unraveling as my two halves are pulled further apart.

36

MY MOTHER WAS a little miffed at having to take the time out from her busy food-shopping schedule in order to pick up the two casualties of the wrath of Stevens's biggest defensive tackle, but when the principal explained that we were completely innocent in the matter (as a bunch of onlookers who so desperately wanted a free psychic session or an invite to my party could attest), she softened and said she would be right over after she got the ice cream into the freezer.

So Scab was suspended, and Pip and I have the day off to recuperate. Nurse Jean, an old lady who is obviously a pacifist, considering the number of times she made "tsk, tsk" noises and shook her head with disapproval, gave Pip an ice pack for his swollen jaw, while I got a little Band-Aid for my nose. It turned out that it wasn't as bad as it had appeared; it wasn't broken, which saved me another agonizing trip to the emergency room. Instead, the jerk had scratched me, from under one eye to just above my lip, with his lame studded bracelet that he thinks makes him ultratough but actually makes him look like a groupie of one of those eighties hair bands. I text Cam with the news of the fight, and it's fewer than ten seconds before he's standing in the doorway of the nurse's office, breathing hard.

"Damn" is all he can say once he's surveyed the damage.

"Please tell me that means you're going to kick his ass."

"He's definitely off my list," he says.

"What list? The list of people whose asses you're not going to kick?" I ask hopefully.

He shakes his head. "Look at me. He outweighs me by a hundred pounds."

"Can't you—I don't know—turn him into a toad?"

"I can't use my magic like that. Not yet, anyway."

Oh, right. Bummer.

Nurse Jean pokes her head behind the curtain and grins. "Oh, Mr. Browne! I thought that was you."

Nurse Jean is, and probably always will be, in love with Cam. With all his minor football injuries, he visits her constantly, so I wouldn't be surprised if he had her number programmed into his cell phone right next to mine. He gives her a semiwave, a little bashful.

She steps back and inspects him. "Well, well, well. You look just great. You must be following that new diet I gave you. Yes?"

He shrugs, and I find myself fascinated by the fact that even a trained medical professional can't notice his obvious physical changes. While she takes Cam across to discuss the diet, I lean over to Pip. "Why can nobody see what's happening to him except me?"

His eyes widen. "What do you mean?"

"Hello? Among other things, his ears are getting pointy, and nobody's freaked out about it."

"You can see that?"

"Uh-huh. Can't you?"

He gnaws nervously on his fingernail. "Massif knew that Cameron would go through certain changes before he fully inherited his powers, so he put a spell over all humans until his sixteenth birthday, to protect him. He was afraid that . . ."

"I know. That we would discriminate against him the way they do humans. The way they did you. Right?"

He looks worried. "Morgan. He put that spell on *all* humans. You are not supposed to be able to see the changes."

"Well, Massif must have screwed up," I say. "I'm a psychic. I can see things lots of people can't. I can even see Dawn when she's invisible."

"I meant to ask you about that. You really can?"

I nod.

His worried look melts into an uneasy smile. "So, you are an enchantress, after all. In Otherworld, we give that name to any human female with magical powers."

"I guess." I return his smile, my cheeks starting to warm under the weight of his gaze. "Are you saying that if Cam did leave, humans wouldn't notice that, either?"

He nods. "That is a fairly simple spell for Massif. It will be like he never existed."

"But it doesn't sound so simple to me. Everyone loves him. They could never forget about him." I watch Nurse Jean talk to

Cam about adding more protein to his diet for his "athletic and muscular body type," and doubt begins to creep in. "You mean, Mr. and Mrs. Browne, too?"

"Yes."

"But how?" I can just imagine Cam's bedroom miraculously changing into a sewing room overnight, and his image disintegrating from every photo I have of him, as if he never existed. It seems impossible.

"That is why I was sent here."

"You mean, you're supposed to take his place? And people won't notice that?" I ask incredulously.

"That is the plan."

"They really think that his own girlfriend, someone who's known him since birth, wouldn't notice the difference?" I ask indignantly, though uncertainty is creeping in. "They *obviously* don't know anything about love."

As soon as the words leave my mouth, it suddenly makes sense, why I've been having those confusing dreams involving Pip. Pip is Cam's replacement. Pip is meant to take his place, in everything. Seamlessly. As Stevens's starting quarterback. As the Brownes' son. And as my boyfriend. It seems so impossible, and yet, I flash back to the dreams I've had, the confusion. If I could be fooled in my dreams, who's to say I wouldn't be fooled when awake?

"But what about enchantresses?" I blurt out. "I mean, what about people like me? Their spells don't work the same on me. Wouldn't I remember him?"

He shrugs. "Possibly. You might not remember everything, but there would be a chance."

I sink down onto the hard, square pillow on the cot and wonder how that would feel. Would remembering what I had lost make it harder to cope? Or would I be happy, knowing he was there, my own fairy godfather?

Pip catches my bemused expression and says, "But that's nothing to worry about."

"I know, I know. I was just thinking . . . in case the plan doesn't work . . ." I stop myself. "But if it does work, will I remember you?"

He thinks for a second. "I do not know, actually."

"I hope I do," I begin, but I catch myself when I realize that every time I think of Pip, I'll know that he's being tortured in Otherworld because of me. It probably serves me right.

"Have you tried envisioning the plan lately?"

I shake off the mental image of Pip being brutally whipped in Otherworld and say, "No. And I won't. I've sworn off envisioning for now. It was making me crazy."

He smiles. "Taking control of your own destiny?"

"We'll see," I answer. After all, that's only possible when you know exactly what you want out of your life. And I thought I did, but now I'm not so sure.

37

I SHOULD HAVE known that my mother wouldn't drop everything and rush right over. It's a shopping trip we're talking about, and she doesn't mess around where food is concerned. She shows up at two in the afternoon, after I explained three times to Nurse Jean that we only live three blocks away from the school and that it would be perfectly safe to let us out on our own. Nurse Jean, however, doesn't have the same love for me that she does for Cam. "Principal's orders," she'd said all three times, though the last time her voice cracked in exasperation and she looked like she was searching for the nearest medical reference book to throw at me.

So by the time my mother shows up, I'm nearly in a coma from looking at the WHAT SMOKING DOES TO YOUR BODY poster on the wall and watching Pip sleep. His face is like that of a little child without a care in the world, despite the fact that he looks like the war wounded and is destined to be punished even more severely in Otherworld in only three days' time.

"*Marone!* Look at your face!" my mother cries when she parts the curtain. She throws her heavy leather bag on my cot, right on my feet, and puts a hand on Pip's chin, inspecting his jaw.

"Ow, Mom," I say, sliding my feet out from under her purse and massaging them. "You do want me to be able to walk out of here, don't you?"

She ignores me. "How in the world did you get into this mess? And three days before the party!"

"I know. Pictures ruined." I groan, remembering how she had squawked after I came home in an arm brace. "Life as we know it, over."

"I have some pancake makeup," she says, tilting my chin up to the fluorescent light. "It could work."

In the back of my mother's Honda SUV, Pip and I are quiet. But my mother and father both have a knack for saving the world from complete silence. She hums along to her one and only, horribly overplayed Andrea Bocelli CD and, in between, peppers us with exciting stories about her trip to Shop Rite. "Turkey Hill was buy one gallon, get one free, so I thought we could have sundaes tonight." And, "The romaine was very wilted, so I had to get iceberg."

My mother invites Pip for dinner, since Cam has a second assignment tonight. I figure this is a good thing; if fairies obviously don't eat so well, it's only fitting that he have a really great meal on one of his last nights on Earth. "Just make sure you pronounce it *pasta fazool*," I whisper to him. "My mother has a thing with pronunciation."

He nods and then leans toward the front of the car. *"Molte grazie, Signora Sparks. Mi piacerebbe visitare l'Italia un giorno di questi."*

My mother perks up right away. *"Prego, prego!"* she bubbles. What is she talking about? Isn't that a brand of pasta sauce that has been banned from our house? When she sees the way he gobbles up her pasta, I'll be surprised if she doesn't offer to divorce Dad and move in with him right away. Meanwhile, Andrea Bocelli is moaning something about *amore*. I wait for Marlon Brando to appear and make me an offer I can't refuse. I stare at Pip, openmouthed, as he goes on conversing with my mom in a language I've never been interested in understanding.

Until now.

When we get home, my mother beams at him and pats his uninjured cheek. Then she says something in Italian to both of us, seemingly forgetting that I have no freaking clue what she is saying. I look at Pip, helpless.

"She wants us to wash up for dinner. It will be ready soon."

"Oh. Um, so, where did you learn Italian?"

He slings his backpack over his shoulder and takes mine from me before I can pull it out of the car. "We had to learn to speak all the languages."

"All?" I ask, doubtful. "So, like, Swahili?"

"Ndiyo," he says hurriedly, maybe to stop me from staring at him with an open mouth, like a freaky blowfish. "Let's go inside. I am quite hungry."

At dinner, it's more Italian. My father minored in Italian in college when he was dating my mother, so he even interjects a word or two. I'm starting to feel like *I'm* the person who's new to the

{187}

world, like *I'm* the outcast. "Can we please speak English?" I finally say, as nicely as possible, so that Pip doesn't think I'm a total brat.

"I'm sorry, hon. But it isn't often I get to practice. And, Pip, you have flawless intonation." She bats her eyelashes at him and then returns to me. "How is the pasta?"

Pip doesn't seem to care about making a fool of himself in front of me. He says, "Fantastic!" with his mouth full, a little elbow of pasta glued to his chin with sticky orange sauce. At times like this, I can really see what lures the girls in.

Speaking of which, his date with Sara had been in the back of my mind all day, but, with all that had happened today, I couldn't find a clever way to bring it up. Now seems as good a time as any. "So, Pip," I begin casually, "how did your date go last night?"

I must be able to pull off "casual," because he doesn't appear to detect anything strange. He simply wipes his mouth with a napkin and says, "Just fine. She is a great person."

I should have expected vagueness from Pip, the ultimate gentleman. I was hoping for something a little more informative: (a) places visited, (b) topics conversed about, (c) bodily fluids exchanged. Considering what I know about Pip, the answers to the above are probably: (a) the diner, (b) the weather, (c) zilch. But why does it still bug me? Why should I care about a guy who isn't even going to be around three days from now?

Maybe it's because I know he's my "replacement boyfriend." Like with a spare tire, even though I don't plan on using him, I don't want anyone else using him, either.

"You had a date!" my mother exclaims, as if Pip were her own child. "How nice."

My father leans back in his chair after polishing off his third plate, so that his shirt stretches over his big belly almost to the point of popping. "I want to hear about this fight. The other guy looks worse, right, Pipster?"

"Pipster"? Agh. Why not give him a playful punch, ruffle his hair, and call him "son"? Many times during my life, I've been convinced my father wanted me to be a boy. Cam sort of filled the void, but, since he's been gone, my father must be going through withdrawal.

Pip looks confused. "No, I don't believe so."

My father waits for him to elaborate and, when he doesn't, slinks back with disappointment. He was clearly hoping for something out of the soap operas.

Pip finishes four plates of pasta, something I don't think even my father could manage, and helps to clear and wash the dishes. My father joins in to help, allowing my mother to just sit there, something that we haven't allowed her to do since the Clinton administration. She can't stop giggling like a schoolgirl. Pip stands at the sink, towel draped over his shoulder, speaking more Italian, and I find myself wondering for the millionth time today how he acted with Sara when they were out together. Of course he was sweet and chivalrous, but did he act different because it was a date? Did he treat her nicer, give her extra special attention? Did he want to kiss her?

The thought puts a knot in my stomach. I mean, what difference does it make? Cam and I are together, and Pip's going off to Otherworld. Replacement boyfriend not needed, thank you very much. That's the plan. Still, for some reason I swallow and gaze at him, willing him to look back at me so that we can share a knowing, secret glance. But he doesn't.

And only a second passes before I feel guilty for even wanting that.

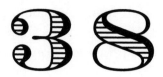

AFTER SCHOOL ON Wednesday, Cam calls me over to his front porch to see his suit. He'd bought it especially for the party, and when he tried it on for the first time, I nearly melted, because he looked so fantastic. Now, standing there on his front porch, he looks kind of like a little kid trying on his daddy's work clothes.

"This looks pathetic." He groans. "I think I'll just let Pip wear it."

"But what will you wear?" I ask, sitting down on the steps.

He shrugs.

"It doesn't matter, anyway. Nobody can see how you've changed. They'll probably think you look amazing in it."

He flexes his knees and peers down at the fabric pooled at his feet. "Not when I trip down the stairs and do a face-plant. These are too big."

"Ohhh-kay, so I am going to be wearing an evening gown, and you are going to be wearing ratty shorts?"

"I'll figure it out."

I eye him suspiciously. "The drill sergeant isn't going to stop you from going to this party, is she? Give you a last-minute assignment?"

"No." He looks out, across the street, and whispers, "The plan is still in effect. I have some things to do tomorrow night, but I'll be good for Friday."

"Okay." I look down at my hands. "And everything's cool? She still thinks you're . . ."

He nods. "Yep."

My mind keeps flashing back to the scars on Pip's back. "You haven't been having any second thoughts?"

He looks into my eyes. "No. Why?"

I try to appear as unconcerned as possible, even though all I can see are those horrible slashes. But no, if Cam is not having second thoughts, then I'm not, either. After all, he's the one giving up his throne for me, the poor commoner. "Nothing. So, are you going to miss the game tomorrow?"

"Yeah." His face stiffens. "There really isn't any point. Plus, I've got a lot of stuff to finish around here."

"They'll probably lose big-time without you and Scab. I don't think I'll go, either."

He kicks the ground with his bare toe. "You heard that Pip is quarterback?"

I snap my eyes to meet his. I don't know why this surprises me. He is, after all, supposed to be Cam's replacement, not just on the field but in life. I haven't seen Pip since we walked to school together this morning, and when he left my side in the parking lot, a couple of A-list seniors from the football team surrounded him. At the moment, I'd thought it was strange, but I figured that maybe they just wanted a blow-by-blow of his fight with Scab. Pip is so mild-mannered and unassuming, but I knew the pass I'd made him throw would make the football team drool with envy. I hadn't imagined this, though. "That's crazy."

"Supposedly, he has one hell of an arm. Who knew?" He slips off the suit jacket and lays it over the back of a lounge chair, then loosens his tie. "John told me the guys got him to try out, and the coach wants him in."

"Wow, does he even know the rules?"

"He'll learn fast. He's inside with Sara right now. She'll teach him that . . . among other things, I am sure." He raises his eyebrows suggestively.

"They are? What does that mean?" I peer into his living room, until I catch a glimpse of my reflection. I look like a demented stalker. I should be happy that Pip and Sara are together for his last days on Earth, but instead, all I'm feeling is jealousy, like the girls who used to drool over Cam. Pathetic. "Pip told me he's supposed to be your replacement. In everything."

This news doesn't surprise him. "I know."

"He was supposed to take your place. As my boyfriend."

I watch for a reaction on his face. Jealousy. Anger. Anything. But there is none. This is clearly something he has known for a while.

"You don't care?"

He looks at the ground, then back at me. "Maybe he was meant to be in my place all along," he says.

I clench my fists. "But he's not. And I love you."

He gives me a slow, sad smile and whispers, "I know. I love you, too. And I'm staying here, so what difference does it make?"

It's just a statement, not a promise. There isn't any resolve in his voice. It frightens me. I catch a glimpse of a bit of wood sticking out from the inside pocket of his suit coat. His chopsti—er, wand. I reach over to grab it and say, "You won't be needing—" The wand falls to the floor and I feel a jolt of electricity run through my fingers. "Ouch!"

"Watch it!" he tells me, a second too late. "Don't touch that."

"I won't, anymore," I say, holding my fingers, which are candy pink and still sizzling. "What the hell?"

He takes the wand and tucks it back into the pocket. "Listen, are you sure you envisioned everything working out?"

"Um, yeah," I lie.

"Okay." He reaches up and pats my head as if he's not substantially shorter than I am, and whispers, "I told her not to hurt you again, but I can't be sure she'll listen to me. So just be good. Okay? Until Friday?"

I heave a sigh and nod. "Whatever."

"No, seriously. I don't want to have to worry about you any more than I already do."

"Okay," I say glumly. "I still don't know why you stick up for her."

He exhales slowly and takes my hand. "I told you. She's not bad. She's just obeying Massif's orders. And she's probably going to catch hell from him if things work out for us. So try to cut her a little slack, okay?"

I throw up my hands. "I know, I know. I am a total brat."

He gives me a quick kiss, and I head across his lawn, through the bushes. As I'm leaving, I see Mrs. Nelson crossing the street, holding the hand of a little platinum-pig-tailed girl. Like my mother had said, she's just as perfect as before—full of life, not frail or pale at all. At first, I think maybe they're coming to see my mother, to thank her once again for the miraculous *sfogliatelle*. Instead, they head off toward the right, and when they reach the curb, the girl breaks free of her mother and runs up the Brownes' driveway. Straight into Cam's waiting arms.

It's strange how kids have always somehow been inexplicably drawn to Cam. But I didn't think he knew Gracie, or the Nelsons—at least, not very well. Gracie has always been a shy kid, ducking behind her mother's legs whenever I would say hello. But now, she's grinning at him like they're the best of friends. She reaches around his back and feels his shoulder blades, and they both break into laughter.

And meanwhile, Mrs. Nelson stands there in the grass. Smiling and wiping her eyes with the back of her hand.

She may be smiling, but she's also sobbing.

And that's when I realize what Cam's "assignments" are.

39

"**M**ORGAN! COME ON, I saved you a seat!" Eden calls from the top row of the bleachers. She's standing there in her green and gold Hawks sweatshirt, and she's wearing one of those atrocious giant foam cowboy hats. She turns toward the center of the gym as the marching band belts out the final few notes of our fight song, and screams a seemingly never-ending "Whoooooooo!"

Reluctantly, I climb up to her seat, noticing two more disgusting purple leech bites on her neck before I plop down and stick my fingers in my ears. Two weeks ago I would have killed to have a pep rally last period instead of English. Now, I think I would so much rather dissect *Leaves of Grass* than sit through this. I see Cam sitting a few rows ahead of me, a blank look on his face. The pink aura is surrounding him, as usual. He's not wearing his jersey, so it's almost like he was never part of the team. I fully expect him to break into tears.

Eden grins and points at me. "Scab gave you a scab."

"Funny."

"What a jerk. I can't believe I missed that," she says glumly. "So, has Cam talked to Scab at all since he was suspended?"

I shake my head. As if Cam has nothing else to worry about.

"Wow. That's so sad! They were, like, best friends."

I shrug, tapping my fingers on the bench. I check the clock. It's two. Time to get this show on the road.

Finally, Principal Edwards strolls up to a podium, and the cheering comes to an end. He lectures, seemingly forever, about how this year's Hawks are going to be the best ever, and I know Cam is wincing at the thought, though I can't see him from my seat. Then he begins to announce the team members.

Eden sways back and forth in her seat and says, "Wow, they really did kick Cam off the team, didn't they?"

I glare at her. "Who told you that? He quit."

She shrugs. "It's the rumor that he lost his arm. Is it true Pip is going to take his place?"

He's not taking his place with me, that's for sure, I think, craning my neck to see the cheerleaders on the sidelines. Sara has her platinum hair in a ponytail and is clapping for a wide receiver. She kicks her pencil-thin leg up so unnaturally high that she can almost kiss her knee. Gross.

"I can't wait for tonight!" she is blabbering as I watch the football players jog out like heroes in their green jerseys, waving and slapping each other on the backside. "You want to meet in the parking lot?"

Eden is obviously so love struck by Mike that she's experiencing delusions. Like I would ever, ever go to this game. After all, my boyfriend was just disgraced into quitting the team. Or maybe he was, like the rumor goes, kicked off. What difference does it make? For the past few years, Cam has lived and breathed football, and now, it's over for him. He's obviously going through a very traumatic period and probably hates everything that has to do with the game. And I need to show my support by boycotting it. I am sure we both would have boycotted this pep rally, too, if it wouldn't have gotten us detention.

Eden is saying something, but it doesn't register until she's halfway through. ". . . really sucks that Cam isn't quarterback anymore, but, like you tell everyone when you tell them futures that aren't exactly great, you have to rise above it. Move on."

I turn to her, ready to spew, and then hold my tongue. She's right, of course. I've used the "move on" speech so often, it's permanently ingrained in my head. But it's easier said than done. I'm about to tell her that, when I realize they're about to announce the starting quarterback.

I'd expected all along to hear his name, but when it's finally out there, I instantly rocket out of my seat, fueled by the energy in the crowd. The applause builds to a roar, and Eden lets out a glass-breaking screech. My eyes go into overdrive, focusing in on the door to the boys' locker room. And there he is, in Cam's number 10 jersey, the Gap jeans I bought for him, and a pair of Nikes. He has a football in the crook of his arm. He won't look up at the crowd, so all I can see is the top of his head, all mussed up, like whipped peanut butter. I blink—can that really be Pip?—and when he takes a few steps, I know the answer.

Swish-swish-swish.

Dragging his feet, he shuffles to the center of the gym. He gives a slight wave but somehow ends up popping the ball out from the cradle of his arm. It rolls onto the floor awkwardly for a moment, and he chases it about before recovering it. There are a few giggles from the audience, but when he waves again, the crowd grows louder. I still can't see his eyes, though. I can't tell if he's excited or scared to death.

Eden whistles and fans her face. "Oh, my God, he is such a hottie. I'll be his tight end any day."

"Whose?"

"Pip's."

I squint at her. I think she said the same thing about Cam a few days ago, around the time she was laughing about the football team stealing Pip's pants.

"These are our Hawks!" Principal Edwards announces to more applause, and the cheerleaders run out to the center of the gymnasium. They all seem to head for Pip, wrapping themselves around him until I can barely locate him in the mob. Then Sara does a cartwheel and bounds over, like a little kitten, pouring herself into his arms. I can see his face now, and there's a smile, a big one I don't think he's ever shown me. She throws her head back and laughs, and he does the same. Have I ever heard him laugh? I watch as, despite the madness around them, they slowly bring their lips together, and—

Gah. What is Cam up to? I quickly switch my gaze to a couple of rows ahead of me, expecting to see him sitting there, silent, a lone tear running down his face.

Instead, he's on his feet, hooting and hollering, pumping

his fist in the air as the pink cloud swirls over his head. Not exactly heartbroken.

Well, he *had* mentioned something about moving on to his next thing. Maybe he's past football. Maybe he's taken up something that his little fairy body will be better able to handle, like crocheting or stamp collecting.

Or maybe something more. Much, much more.

40

'M ON THE porch again, listening to the faraway voices of Laura from *Little House on the Prairie* wafting from my living room. It's another warm night, and before, adults were walking past with strollers and mowing their lawns, and kids were shouting out in play. Even little Gracie was out, with her first pair of roller skates, Mrs. Nelson watching with eyes that never wanted to lose sight of her again. But the sun has long since set, and I'm still outside, still trying to read the first few pages of *Leaves of Grass* for class tomorrow. At this point, I'm one line into the first poem and confused, my mind completely lost on something that was happening only a few streets over.

Over the trees I could even see the glare of the stadium lights, casting the dark sky a gunmetal gray. And I could hear the cheering of the audience every so often in between Laura yelling for Ma or Pa. The crowd cheered a lot, so Pip probably did them proud and won the game. I bet he had the entire student body chanting his name. I'm sure the team picked him up on their shoulders and carried him around the field. Sara probably took him in for a passionate celebratory kiss on the fifty-yard line, while confetti floated around them.

Then the ending credits rolled and they lived happily ever after. Okay, so it probably wasn't that perfect, but the thought still makes me gag.

"Are you okay?"

I whip my head around and see a form standing on my lawn, in the darkness. Cam? It moves through the bushes, and at once, Pip's features come into the light; his golden hair a mess, the purple bruise on his lip just an outline now. He is wearing an oversized Hawks T-shirt that shows off his powerful lower arms, and has a gym bag slung over his shoulder. The bulb overhead glows yellow in each of his eyes, and, since his mouth is still swollen, I can't make out his expression.

"Fine," I answer, straightening. "You won the game, right?"

He nods. "How did you . . . Oh, that's right. Enchantress."

I shake my head. "I didn't envision it. I just knew. But why are you back so soon? Isn't there a celebration at the Parsonage?"

"Yes," he says, climbing the steps to the porch and hefting his heavy bag onto the ground. "But, you know, about tomorrow. I wanted to talk to you about it."

I squelch the desire to hear him tell me, "I rushed right home because I missed you," and say, "That's right. Are you ready?"

I move my bare feet from the glider, and he takes the seat next to me. "Yes. Are you?"

"I just want it to be over with." I sigh. "I think Dawn has been making me think and feel things that aren't real. I don't like it."

He wrinkles his nose. "But you told me you can see Cameron in his true form."

"Well, yeah, but other things . . ."

He looks confused. "That was a very powerful spell that Massif put on us humans, making us see Cameron as he once was. And you can see Dawn, even when she makes herself invisible. If you're immune to those spells, you're probably immune to all Magic of Thought."

"Magic of Thought?"

"Making you perceive things that don't exist, or not perceive things that do."

"I guess, but . . ." I bite my tongue. If I'm immune to Magic of Thought, then the feelings I've had for Pip are . . .

No. No. No.

"So, are you saying, hypothetically," I say, making sure that word is clear, "that a fairy probably couldn't, I don't know, get in your mind and make you think you were in love with someone?"

He laughs. "Not possible. I told you, fairies don't understand that kind of love. They surely couldn't concoct a love spell."

I freeze. My stomach starts to ache. Something inside me isn't working right. I stare at *Leaves of Grass,* unable to meet his gaze. I am an evil, evil girl.

He's going on, oblivious to the heart attack I'm having. "I believe Dawn is aware of everything."

The plan? My heart begins to beat faster, humming like a motor in my chest. "How do you know?"

He sits beside me on the glider and whispers in my ear, his cheek against mine, soft and begging to be kissed. "I came right here because before I left for the game, I heard Dawn talking to Cameron."

"And . . ."

"She told him that if she doesn't deliver him to Otherworld tomorrow night, Massif will kill her." He leans in still closer. "Why would she tell him that, unless she had a reason to believe he might not follow her to Otherworld?"

"Is it true? Will Massif kill her?"

His lips form a straight line. "Possibly."

"And you think that means she knows about our plan?"

"Yes. I think it means she's not going to let you stand in her way. No matter what Cameron says." He's so close that I can smell Cam's scent on his jersey, and it's hard not to lean into him. "She knows that you are the one thing that would make Cam stay in this world. If you're gone, he will have no reason to stay here."

I break out of the daze and suddenly feel cold. I'd imagined that maybe she would lock me in a basement until Cam was safely in Otherworld. Perhaps make it so that my mom's SUV broke down on the way to the party. But this . . . this means . . .

"You think she's going to try to kill me?"

He nods.

"But how? You said I'm immune to her magic."

His face is stone. "That doesn't make you invincible."

"No, of course not. But Cam wouldn't let that happen. He said he would kill her if she hurt me."

"Dawn's only mission in life is to deliver him to Otherworld. She will die if she doesn't make this happen. And I doubt Massif would allow Cameron to harm her. He wants their kingdoms to unite."

"But if I'm dead, Cam would never go back to Otherworld. He'd hate Dawn forever. He'd stay here, just out of spite."

He shakes his head. "I don't think he would."

Anger wells inside me. "How do you know? You don't know Cam."

"But I do know what it is like to be different, to be an outcast," he says softly. "And if Cameron stays here past his sixteenth birthday, Massif will no longer protect him. His spell will be broken. The one he put over all humans. The one you are immune to."

"So, everyone will see him as he is? Wings and ears and . . . everything?"

He nods.

My heart stops.

"Cam doesn't care how he looks," I say, but even as the words come out, I know that he does. After all, that was the reason he'd been moping about day after day, feeling useless. But would he really rather spend an eternity married to a demented fairy than live in this world? If I weren't around to protect him, maybe. "And what about his powers?"

"They will be gone."

I bite my tongue. The only thing that has made Cam smile in the past few days is the fact that he's found his next thing. That he is useful. Would he really want to give that up for me? Wouldn't he be crazy to even consider that?

Finally, I ask, "Do you think we shouldn't go through with this?"

"No, not at all." And then those eyes, afire in the light from above, focus on me, completely serious and warning. "But I want you to be safe."

I swallow, breathless. I do a mental inventory and realize that the only thing between me and a painful death is a powerless fairy and a guy who has been known to pee his pants at the sight of anything with wings. Not good. I shiver, wishing I'd taken some sort of martial arts course.

"I just want everyone to be happy," I murmur. "And it seems like, whatever happens, someone is going to suffer."

Pip notices that I'm trembling and puts an arm around my shoulder. It feels nice, and strangely familiar. He looks across the street, into the black night. "What—" he begins. It's a full minute before he starts up again. "What thoughts were you having? The ones you believed the fairies were making you think?"

"Um. Nothing." As if I'd ever let him know about those. Goose bumps appear on my arms, and I have to rub them away. "What do you think about this? Do you think Cam can still be happy here?"

"Of course. He has you."

"But he won't have any powers. He'll be five feet tall, with pointed ears and wings. And completely useless."

"Fairies rarely grow over four feet tall," he points out.

I sigh. "Even better. At first, Cam might be okay with it. But eventually, it will eat away at him. People are cruel to those who are different. You know that."

"But he will still have you."

Yes, but will he? What if Dawn is planning something? What if she is planning to kill me?

Pip gives me a cautious smile, then stands and hefts his bag higher onto his shoulder. "Watch out for yourself, enchantress. And keep your windows closed tonight."

The way he says it, it makes me shiver. I watch him disappear into the darkness between the bushes, then kick aside *Leaves of Grass* and stare up at the blue-black sky. Out of the corner of my eye, I think I see a pink aura floating in the light of the porch. When I turn to face it, it's gone.

And something tells me it's going to be a very long night.

41

LYING IN BED, I listen to the rain pattering against the window. I roll over and pull up the covers, feeling the pillow against my back. Though it's soft and lifeless and cool to the touch, since all my dreams were filled with him—holding me, stroking my arms—it almost feels like he's there with me. And maybe that's why, despite the stern warning Pip gave me last night, I felt safe.

Today is October 15. My birthday. My sweet sixteen. The day I am finally supposed to be a woman.

I'd so hoped womanhood would bring wisdom.

Of course it would be raining today. Never mind that my hair is going to be a frizz fest by the time the party is in full swing. In less than fourteen hours, one of the men of my dreams will be gone forever.

I can only hope that when it's all over, I'm more relieved than sad.

I'm still wiping sleep out of the corner of my eyes when I come downstairs and nearly trip over a large brown mass at the foot of the steps. In a flash, I wonder if Dawn had placed an obstacle in my way in a lame attempt to kill me. But then I realize it's my mother, scrubbing the hardwood floors. I expect a bright and cheery birthday greeting, but instead she bears down all her weight on the sponge, drops it into the bucket, and huffs, "*Marone!* These floors are a mess." There's a wild, unfocused look in her eyes.

My mother's cleaning fits are like her shopping trips—completely, psychotically elevated to the importance and difficulty of rocket science. She's gone off the deep end before, usually before company comes. "Mom, you know that nobody's coming here. Everyone will be at the Toad."

"But what if someone wants to come back for coffee," she says, more as a statement than a question, surveying the rest of the floor. "Go in the kitchen and get your orange juice. Take off your shoes first."

I'm about to argue that the party will run way late, and we'll have plenty of coffee at the Toad, but then I decide it's pointless. I pull off my boots, one by one, and trudge down the hall in my pink socks, not feeling much like orange juice. Not feeling much like anything, actually, knowing there's a possibility Dawn could slip some cyanide into it to get me out of the way.

And that's when I see him, standing in the middle of the kitchen. At first I see only his feet, but my eyes trail upward, past the sea of too-baggy clothes he's swimming in, right to an enormous bouquet of pink- and red-foil chocolate roses. He's known forever that I think flowers are a waste and chocolate is the food of the gods. It's comical, because he's now so short, nearly a foot shorter than I am, and his face is so hidden that it's almost like the flowers have legs. "Happy birthday," the talking bouquet says.

I feel a pang of guilt, a sudden desire to climb up to my room and hide there, away from Pip and Cam and my divided feelings, forever. Instead, I take a step forward.

"Happy birthday to you, too," I say, both elated and sad that he knows me so well. I take the flowers from his hands and look down at him, then stoop over awkwardly, and . . . kiss the top of his head, as if I'm his grandma. I never thought anything with Cam could be this weird. "They're nice."

My mother comes up behind me and says, "Well, don't wait. Give him your gift."

"My—oh." I'd bought it at the Menlo Park Mall last month, though it seems like ages ago. It's been in my bag ever since, and at first I couldn't wait to give it to him, it was so perfect. But so much has changed. I fumble around in my knapsack and pull it from the bottom, a gum wrapper stuck to it. "I bought it before—well, before," I explain.

"Thanks, Boo." He takes the small package in his delicate hands, carefully slits the tape, and pulls off the very masculine blue and gold wrapping. "Wow. Amazing."

"My parents chipped in," I say. "We knew how much you wanted it."

He had wanted a wristwatch for years. In school, they are nearly unheard of, but Cam had read somewhere that a man with a wristwatch looks infinitely more intelligent and put together. So my mother and I had decided to buy him a really nice one from Macy's. But now I'm not sure he'll use it. Still, he holds it in both hands and grins. "Thanks to both of you."

"Try it on, try it on," my mother bubbles, giving him a don't-mention-it wave.

He removes it from the package, loosens the clasp, and slides it over his bony wrist. When he closes it, I can see the gigantic gap between the metal and his skin. As soon as he tilts his arm to show it off, the watch falls to the ground and skitters across the linoleum.

"What—" my mom begins, confused. "Is the closure broken?"

Under the spell, I suppose the glossy silver watch looked just glorious on his wrist. I can remember those muscles in his arms, his powerful forearms, and those worn, big hands of his, but it's fuzzy now, which is sad, because I thought I'd know everything about him by heart forever. Part of me envies my mother's ignorance and wishes I could see the old Cam again, even if it isn't real.

"No, it's great," Cam says, picking up the watch and placing it back in the case. "Probably just needs some adjustment."

"Off to school for you," my mom says casually, giving me a shove. "I can't have you messing with my floors anymore."

I glare at her.

She tries to glare back, but she's no good at bluffing. "Happy birthday, sweetheart," she says, handing me a card.

I grin and open it. It's a really flowery one about how I'm a wonderful daughter and have blossomed so nicely into woman-hood. It's a little corny, but I wipe a tear from my eye and give her a hug. "Thanks, Mom."

That's the end of the gift giving, since the trade-off was agreed to months ago. Nice gift or big party. I'd known a car was out of the question, since I won't get my license until next year, so it made it pretty easy to decide on the party. Plus, with Cam going in on it, it sounded like a fantastic way to celebrate.

Now it doesn't seem so fantastic.

Considering the prospect of losing Cam forever or sending Pip back into a world where he'll be tortured and ridiculed—not to mention a demented fairy on the loose—tonight sounds downright scary.

"Ready for school?" Cam asks me as I finish wiping my eyes and prop the card up on the kitchen table. When he takes my hand with the tips of his small, bony fingers, I know he can't be much of a bodyguard anymore. In fact, his body is made for only one purpose, and after tonight, if all goes as planned, he won't even have that.

The thought makes me feel more sad and vulnerable than ever.

42

"THANKS FOR SCARING me to death," I mumble to Pip when I get him alone. "I hardly slept at all last night because I was so worried Dawn would murder me."

"I'm sorry, Morgan." That's when I notice his eyes are red-rimmed. He yawns.

"You were up, too? Watching me?" I ask, thinking about the dreams I'd had when I finally fell asleep. In them, he was there with me. I'd felt safe.

He says nothing, just plays with his sleeve.

"So you were."

We're in the hallway at school. A bunch of girls walking behind us call out a happy birthday to me. I smile and thank them but quickly turn my attention back to Pip.

He says, "I told you, I want you to be safe."

I'm both flattered and a little disgusted. But it's Pip we're talking about. His intentions are pure, I'm sure. "Okay. So are you going to follow me around all day?"

He nods. "Unless you don't want me to."

"I don't want you to miss class." But, then again, I don't really want to die, either.

"Okay. Well, I will check in on you throughout the day." He grins at me. His smile melts me.

By the time I leave school, Pip has checked in on me so much that he's a step away from being my shadow. And it's a good thing, too, because my brain is so scattered, Dawn wouldn't need to use magic to do me in. There's so much on my mind, I'm having trouble keeping my balance. Tense images and fragments of past conversations float in and out: Cam's bright smile after his first fairy assignment. Those horrible, horrible scars on Pip's back. His white-blue eyes, like a summer sky filled with gauzy clouds, focusing on me with complete intensity.

Cam walks me back from school, and for the first time, as we huddle under the extrawide umbrella he brought with him, I end up carrying my own books. He looked so silly, like a leprechaun toting two heavy sacks of gold to the rainbow.

"You look freaked. What's up?" he asks me as we're walking down our street.

"Just nervous about the party. I don't want to trip during our grand entrance," I fib.

He switches his bag to the other shoulder; he's having trouble carrying his own load. "You're not worried about the other thing. The plan?"

"A little."

"Pip and I will do the best we can to protect you," he whispers, his face serious. "But you know I don't fully inherit my powers until midnight. Until then, she's stronger than I am. And if you're in danger . . . plan aborted."

I nod, hoping it doesn't come to that. Cam is so tiny now, without magical powers, he's about as vulnerable as a newborn fawn. "Is that all you're worried about? What about tomorrow? And the future?"

He stops and looks at me; then his eyes trail away. "I don't care about that."

Liar, liar. As different as he has become, the funny thing is, I still know what's inside. I still know him.

A few minutes of silence, and we're in front of his house. "You better go take a shower and get ready," I tell him. "We're leaving here at six sharp."

He rolls up the roomy sleeve of his shirt and shows me a dozen small red blisters on the underside of his hand, like drops of rain. "I think I have to skip the shower from now on."

I take his hand gently and look closer. "Are you serious? That's from water?"

"Yeah."

I quickly move the umbrella over him. If he can't even survive a rainstorm, if he can't ever take a simple shower . . . how will his life in this world be? "I should have bought you a bubble instead of a watch," I say lightly, forcing my grimace into smile territory before he can pick up on it.

I look across the street, where Gracie is wearing a ladybug rain slicker and splashing through puddles of water from the downspouts under the eaves of her house. "I know what you did for her," I say quietly. "For Gracie? You're her fairy godfather, aren't you?"

He looks at her, and a smile spreads across his face. "Well, sort of. It's amazing, isn't it?"

"I'll say. So that's why you've been so happy."

He can't help grinning madly. It's the first I've seen a smile like that in a while. "She was so fragile. So sick. They thought she would be gone in another few days. And I visited her in the hospital. All I had to do was talk to her. And that was it." He's looking at his hands as if he can't believe the power in his own body. "And yesterday I reunited a lady with her children. They'd been kidnapped and—"

"You're going to lose those powers if you stay here," I say.

He frowns. "I know."

"You'll be miserable here."

He's silent for a moment, still looking at his hands, those smooth, dainty hands. "But I'll have you," he says weakly.

"You'll be miserable here," I repeat, putting a hand on his shoulder. "And Massif is going to kill Dawn if you stay. You care about her, don't you?"

He looks off into the distance, at nothing in particular, and takes a breath.

"I know you do. You don't have to lie. It's okay."

"But I love you, Boo. And I don't want to leave you."

Holding the umbrella tightly in my hands, I come up close to him. I have to stoop a bit, but, surrounded by his big UCLA sweatshirt, which is laced with his old, familiar smell, I feel comfortable. His lips, fortunately, are no different than they've ever been, and when he kisses me, everything seems right. This seems right.

But I can't shake the feeling that this kiss is our last.

{215}

43

I CLOSE MY eye and, for the twelfth time in an hour, try to glue a fake-eyelash piece to my lid. It slips and ends up attached to my nostril. Another tear mixes with my eyeliner and creates a black wading pool in the corner of my eye. The pancake makeup has covered the remnants of the scratch Scab gave me, but the tears keep flubbing up the artistry. If my mother knew I was crying and making myself look like an extra from *Prom Night Massacre* on the special event she's sunk so much of her cash into, she'd probably kick my sorry ass. Still, stepping back, I look like I should be rifling through garbage cans. Thankfully, the gorgeous silver strapless dress with the teal bow, and the strappy sandals, help elevate me slightly from the slums.

When I'm done, I walk silently out of my room, head down,

not feeling anything close to what a princess must feel like. This is not what I'd imagined this night would be. The light is on in my parents' room and I can smell my mother's perfume, so I know they're getting ready, and it'll be just moments before my mother is sounding the battle cry for us to report to the foyer for inspection. So I grab the shawl I've borrowed from my mother and, since the rain has nearly stopped, trudge across to the gazebo in our garden. All the plants are depressingly brown and sagging with rainwater, which may contribute to the fact that as soon as I get inside and close the screen door, I burst into tears.

Why did I bring up Gracie? Why did I push a confession out of him? If I didn't, he wouldn't be having any second thoughts; he'd just follow the plan. Now, he's thinking about how completely miserable he's going to be here, all because I had to bring it up. And the fact is, I know he's going to be miserable if he stays with me. I know it. And maybe I brought it up because above all, I want him to be happy. But I still don't want to be without him. I don't want Cam to leave me. Does that make me selfish?

The screen door creaks open. I expect it to be my mother, launching into a "Look at your mascara!" rampage, but instead my eyes trail up Pip's tall form, his elegant black suit and blue satin tie. I gulp when I see him standing there.

He doesn't say a word, just comes inside and sits carefully beside me. I feel his arm snake under my shawl, around my bare shoulders, and as I let my head fall against his chest, I inhale the scent that once was Cam's. Somehow that makes me cry harder. I cover my face so that I don't schmutz up his suit with my tears. Finally, I pull back and sniffle, "Oh, happy birthday."

His body trembles a little, and I know he's laughing. "Same to you."

I can't help laughing a little, too, through the tears. "The happiest," I say.

We're silent for a few minutes. Finally, I whisper into his suit jacket, "I guess you're wondering why I'm crying."

"I think I know."

"Everything is working against us," I sniffle. "Sometimes I think he has to leave me, that that is the only way he'll be happy."

"I'm sure he doesn't want to leave you."

"We've been together since forever. He might be able to go on without me," I sob, "but I know I can't do it. I can't be without him. He says I'm brave, but the truth is, I'm not. Without him, I'm not."

He doesn't say anything, just rubs his hand up and down my arm, gently.

I look up, and his eyes meet mine. In the gloom and shadows, I can barely see his irises; they're just black, but somehow still warm. "You have to help me. We have to convince him to stay."

He nods. "I will do whatever you say."

"I know. I love that about you," I sniffle. Through it all, I have always been able to rely on him to never go back on his word. Here I am, about to send him back to Otherworld, his own personal hell, and he's still faithful. "But why?"

He looks at the ground. "Why what?"

"Why are you so good to me?"

"Because . . . ," he begins, and I know exactly what he's going to say.

"Yeah, yeah, yeah. True love," I say, pulling the shawl tighter. Suddenly, it's very cold. "But maybe you should stop worrying about what others want and start caring about what you want. You have to stop thinking you don't matter."

He shrugs. "In Otherworld, I don't."

"But you do! I've never met anyone so selfless and sweet in all my life!" I protest. Is it possible that only a week ago, he was this gawky little boy from another planet? Now, he's so beautiful, I have a hard time looking him in the eye without blushing. And when he's close to me, like he is now, and the only sound is the rain falling all around us, I can't seem to think of anything other than having him closer. Is it just me, or does he feel it, too? I can't tell, but he is breathing hot on my cheek, and I smell the grass, and peppermint from his toothpaste, which makes me woozy. Soon I find myself moving inexplicably toward his lips, reaching up to meet them with mine. . . .

The screen door to the gazebo opens, and I jump clear off the bench. My mother is standing there with an umbrella, her black hair piled on her head, the collar of her black raincoat high against her ears. "Jesus, this weather," she growls to herself, and as she focuses on me, her eyes turn to slits. "There you are. I've been calling for you for twenty minutes. Let's get a move on."

I stand up obediently, wondering if my face is completely ruined. Since my mother has us getting into the city a full hour ahead of schedule, "in case of traffic," I'm sure there will be time for touch-ups, or in my case, complete makeovers, once we get to the Toad. At least, I hope.

"Oh! Mr. Pip!" My mother's tone turns to hostess. "How nice to see you."

"Thank you, Mrs. Sparks," he says, always the gentleman.

"Cameron isn't here with you?" she asks, searching the small space to be sure, as if we'd hidden him under the bench.

"No, he must still be at his house," I say.

Pip is still gazing at me. He mouths the words "It's okay."

But I have a hard time believing that's true.

44

SMOKEY JOE THE DJ, a guy who looks about eighty but is dressed like a homey, is setting up, and Gizelle is milling importantly around the room, nodding and pausing every so often to scribble on a clipboard. I can't tell if anything is missing, since all I can remember about the evening is that the tables are supposed to be set with silver napkins. Or was it teal?

I need some alone time. As soon as we pile out of my mom's SUV, I make a beeline for the bathroom with my makeup bag. My mother doesn't try to stop me. She must have been too frazzled by the upcoming party or awed by Pip's sexiness to notice at the gazebo, but while I was getting into the car, she clasped her hand over her mouth. I've been dreaming about this evening for months, and "What the hell happened to your face?" isn't exactly the comment I've envisioned people making about me.

Inside, I see what all the shock and trauma was about. I look like a bomb went off in front of me, so I have to scrub my cheeks vigorously and start again. I pull my hair back into the updo with about a hundred bobby pins, press some pancake makeup into the scratch Scab gave me, and start to look normal again. But as I'm about to apply eyeliner to my top lid, it hits me.

For the first time in my life, I wanted to kiss someone other than Cam.

My fingers slip, and I write a line of brown kohl across my temple, straight into my hairline. Blast.

Why? Was that me getting back at Cam for even thinking about leaving me? Was it all just retaliation?

I take a tissue and moisten it under the tap, then erase away the line. No, that's not it. I've been having feelings for Pip, odd, unexplainable feelings, for almost a week. I've been chalking them up to fairy magic, but the fact is, those feelings are real.

I really am attracted to Pip.

Not good. Definitely *not* a good thing.

Stepping away from the mirror, I reapply my lip gloss and then frown at myself. I look gorgeous, at last.

But why do I feel so horrible?

Out of the corner of my eye, I see someone walk into the room. I expect the person to go into a stall, but I'm so swept up in my thoughts that I don't notice, after a full minute, that the form is still standing in the doorway, unmoving. Staring at me through the mirror. Finally, I look up and meet her gaze, and swallow hard.

Dawn.

She's dressed in a stunning pink party dress. Standing next to her in the mirror, I look like a Fashion Don't. She smiles at me, then tosses a small gold bag on the counter and runs a finger under her flawless doe eye. "I don't know about you," she says, "but I am ready to party."

I want to tell her that I don't remember extending her an invite, but my mouth is frozen. Because for the first time, the fear Pip feels when he's around Dawn is rubbing off on me. I'm alone, and completely helpless. Would anybody be able to hear me if I screamed? The party is still an hour away. She could end my life right here, and nobody would be able to stop her.

Finally, I catch my breath. "I guess you must be happy. Tonight's the night you get Cam."

"Yes." Her smile transforms into an evil scowl as I attempt to look as innocent as possible. I know it isn't working; my face is burning red, and I have to look away from her intense glare. "With or without your help."

I have to clamp my mouth shut to keep my teeth from chattering. "What does that mean? You've won. He wants to go with you now."

At this point, that probably isn't a lie.

She smiles, almost warmly. "Of course he does. He has no reason to stay here. But, you see, there is one issue that is troubling me. We only have one opportunity to make sure Cameron returns to his throne in the Seelie Court, and I can't take any chances. I need to do everything in my power to ensure he crosses over as planned, even if it means removing certain 'possibilities.' Do you understand what I am saying?"

I nod numbly.

"You see, I get the feeling he still thinks he has a reason to stay."

"And you think that reason is me."

"It is unfathomable that he would give up his royal birthright for a common human, but it seems so." Her eyes narrow. "You think you're so clever because you can somehow see me when other humans cannot. But you're still just a human. You'll never be a match for us."

I clench my fists and steel myself, feeling jealousy burning in my chest. She obviously hasn't been in this world long enough to realize that all the fairy magic in the world couldn't rival the venom of an angry Italian. "Look. I know that you're just under orders. And I know you'll die if you don't deliver Cam back to Otherworld. So I understand why you're getting so, um, intense. But really . . . Cam wants to go."

She smiles again. "Why don't I believe you?" She looks into the mirror, adjusts a wisp of platinum hair behind her ear, and sneers, "Oh, I know. Because right now, that pathetic human slave boy is out on the balcony, trying to coax Cameron to stay."

I freeze, feel a trickle of sweat sliding down my rib cage.

"And I wonder who put him up to that?" She faces me, putting her hands on her hips. "The answer is obvious. That slave has been infatuated with you forever. He used to watch you constantly from Otherworld, longing to be in Cameron's place."

I swallow. "He did?"

Her eyes widen. "Oh, you didn't know that? He thinks it should have been his. But the fact is, he's no match for Cameron. Even you wouldn't want him."

I shake my head vehemently. "That's not true."

She smiles, satisfied. "I know." Her eyes bore into me. "It doesn't explain, though, why you were planning on sending him back in Cameron's place."

I bite my lip. I guess we were no match for the fairies.

"Do you think I didn't know what you were whispering about?"

I feel my fingernails digging into my palms, and my knees tremble. "Well, then, why don't you just kill me now?"

Not wanting to give her any ideas or anything.

"I made a promise to Cameron that I wouldn't kill you," she says, shaking her head as if she wished she hadn't and would love to squeeze her hands around my throat.

I breathe a sigh of relief.

"But," she says softly, moving so close to my cheek that I feel compelled to take a step backward, "there are other ways. You humans have many weaknesses that we fairies do not have."

I stare at her, not quite getting what she means. "As in?"

She ignores me. "And perhaps not only will they help me achieve my goal of making Cameron our king, but they will also have the added advantage of making you regret every last day you spend in this world. And that would be quite satisfying, I think."

She can't kill me for trying to keep Cameron here, but maybe . . . maybe she would just maim me? I shrink against the cold, tiled wall, preparing for the blow.

Instead, she simply tosses her hair. "Glad we had this talk," she says, striding out the door.

I turn back to the sink and my reflection, my skin now ashen under the blush I just applied. My hands are shaking so much that they can't even hold on to the edge of the counter for support. I'm not sure I remember how to breathe.

45

I STAY ALONE in the restroom until the guests start to arrive. The good thing is that Dawn probably won't harm me if I stay here, out of the way of her "plan," but the bad thing is that my mother *will* if I spend the entire party in the lav. I must have left my cell at home in all the confusion, so the only reason I know that it's after nine is that while I'm sitting in a stall, hoping to avoid Pip, Cam, and Dawn as much as possible for the next four hours, two girls walk in who sound suspiciously like Jacinta and Janella Cruise. They're seniors that Cam insisted on inviting because they've dated just about every senior on the football team at one time or another, so, in his eyes, they're considered part of the Hawks football family. In my eyes, they're skanks. Pathetic football groupies. Not to mention that they're both as dumb as stumps. But I guess I was in a forgiving mood when we put the guest list together all those months ago.

They go into stalls on either side of me, chattering away like they'll blow up if they stop talking for even ten seconds. The one on the right—I can't tell which, because not only do they look completely alike, they both have identical high-pitched voices that can grate cheese—says, "Oh. My. God. Did you hear about Sierra?"

Who hadn't heard about Sierra? The only truly shocking thing here would be if Jacinta and Janella actually knew how to pronounce "Harvard."

They both start to pee at exactly the same time, which is just plain freaky, as the one to the left of me squeaks, "No, whuh?" Obviously talking and peeing at the same time is a challenge for her.

Righty says, "Oh. My. God. It's so, like. Horrible. Like. She was, like, caught cheating on her calculus exam. Like, seriously!"

Lefty gasps. "Seriously? Like. Oh. My. God!"

I'd been doodling on a piece of toilet paper with my eyeliner, but I stop and stand up. They both flush at the same time (of course), and they're such powerful flushes, I find myself willing the toilets to quiet down so that I don't miss any of the conversation.

"She must, like, be in sooooo much trouble."

They're washing their hands at the sink. One of them gets a hold of some aerosol hair spray and starts to spray it, continuously, for about three minutes. This does nothing to help me distinguish between the two, because both Janella and Jacinta have notoriously crispy hair.

"Like, yeah. Like, I think they expelled her or something. Like, so, goodbye, graduation. Goodbye, future. Goodbye–"

"Harvard," I say to myself, dazed. Hello Middlesex Community College. So my vision . . . wasn't wrong?

A full ten seconds pass before I realize they've gone completely silent.

"Like. Who's in there?" one of them shouts through the closed door.

Damn, had I said that aloud?

I stand there, very still and silent, hoping that their tiny minds, which can only focus on one thing at a time, will move on to the pretty soaps shaped like ducks on the sink.

"Like, show yourself," the other says, standing firm.

"No comprendo," I say softly. *"Baja en el ascensor."*

A few more seconds of silence. "Like, that means they ate too much cheese," one finally says.

"Ew. Like, let's get out of here."

Their heels go clip-clopping along the marble, toward the door. "Did you see Cam? He's like, the hottest . . ." is the last thing I hear before their voices trail out of earshot.

I release the lever and slowly open the door, still thinking about Sierra. I know that this time next year, she'll probably be walking to class on the Middlesex Community College campus.

And I know that my visions are always, always right.

Pip is staying here with me.

My reflection stares back at me, wide-eyed and unsure. Before the prospect of losing Cam existed, I'd never looked so pathetic. I was tough. I took no prisoners. If a fairy wanted to hurt me, I'd tell her where to go, without the help of any guy. And I'd never question my feelings, ever.

Pip is staying here with me. Cam is going to be king of Otherworld. That is the way it is supposed to be.

For the first time, I think that maybe, just maybe, everything will be all right.

I squint at myself and whisper, "Time to take control of your destiny." Then I press my lips together to get my lip gloss on evenly, make sure the posts of my earrings are on securely, smooth out the front of my dress, open the door, and step outside.

46

E DEN IS THE first person to greet me when I come out. "Greet," though, is too nice a word. She nearly mows me down on the way to the restroom. She's wearing the nice orange chiffon dress we picked out at Macy's together that works so well with her red hair. I expected she'd put her corkscrews into an updo, but they're all down around her shoulders, and rather rat's-nesty. And I don't think she has any makeup on at all. If she'd only been here an hour ago, when I was in the midst of my breakdown, I would have been in good company.

"Morgan," she mutters, not at all glad to see me. It's a total 180 from the giant cupcake and early-season *American Idol* rendition of "Happy Birthday" she presented me with earlier in the day. She seems dazed, so it doesn't surprise me when she blinks twice at me and says, again, "Morgan."

"Yeah, that's me," I say, and immediately I know exactly what is on her mind. Mike Kensington. Either he broke up with her or maybe she saw him with another guy, but the fact of the matter is, I was right.

Again.

Yeah, baby.

"Mike?" I ask simply.

A tear slides down her cheek as she nods ever so subtly. "Why didn't you tell me?" she moans.

I put my arms around her. "Oh, hon. I'm sorry."

We stand there for a while, just hugging each other. I feed her paper towels until the tide of tears ebbs.

"Look," I say, wrapping my arm around her shoulders and leading her away from the bathroom. We're in the lobby, surrounded by funky sculptures of native Africans with spears, when I whisper, "Do you know John Vaughn?"

"Who?"

The guy has been following her around like a puppy for weeks, and yet she has no clue.

"He's cute. He's been asking about you forever. You should go dance with him."

"Uh, okay," she says as I lead her into the room.

It's dark, and the music is raging. The room looks like one of the city's most happening clubs. A bunch of people come up to me and say happy birthday, and how the party is kickin', so I guess I could have spent all night in the ladies' room and it wouldn't have made any difference. The room is so packed and dark that everyone seems pressed together like one big people sandwich, and I can barely make out a soul.

Dawn is nowhere in sight, or else I'm sure the male half of the student body would be crowding around her. And normally, Cam would have stood head and shoulders above everyone. Now, he's completely lost among the bodies. At least, to me he is. "Eden, do you see Cam?" I ask.

She's giving me a "duh" look in the light of the strobe. "Yeah, right there. You need to get the prescription on your contacts checked."

She points toward the DJ, and I still can't see him, so I move forward a little, until I catch John and some of his other football buddies, standing together on the edge of the dance floor. They look as if they're standing beside a swimming pool, testing the water, deciding whether to jump in. As I move around the bodies, I finally notice him, looking so small and delicate next to the big boys, it's scary. One of them could step on him, squash him, and barely notice.

"Perfect," I say, then break into the crowd. "John, you know Eden. Eden, this is John. Go dance."

They look at each other for a moment, and then John shrugs. Eden shrugs back, and they're off. This is how some of the greatest matches in the history of the world were made, I'm sure. I'd expect them to name their first child after me if I weren't now so certain that my vision of her talking to her Precious Moments figurines was right.

Cam flashes a hollow smile up at me, looking nervous. Who can blame him? At the stroke of midnight, his life is going to change forever. "Having fun?" I ask.

"Yeah. You?"

"We need to talk," I say. "Badly."

"I know."

The words are still coming out of his mouth when my mother taps me on the shoulder. "There you are, hon!" she says brightly, though I can tell it's just her hostess's cover for massive annoyance. "We've been looking all over for you. We'd like to get some pictures. Come along."

I give him a worried look as she pulls me away. A group of girls immediately surround him, asking for a dance, though every one of them is nearly twice his size. He moves between them and mouths the words, "Back balcony. Eleven-thirty?"

"Okay," I say, wondering if thirty minutes is going to be enough to sort this all out. I needed more time than that to pick the napkins.

47

MY MOTHER GETS me in every conceivable pose suitable for a sweet sixteen, every one of them increasingly corny, like holding a rose, fixing my hair, and her famous "Look back to yesterday," where I have my hands on my hips, head turned, and am glancing over my shoulder. I never should have let my father buy that digital camera for her birthday last year. I complain that I'm missing out on my own party, but she keeps saying, "One day you'll look back at these pictures and thank me." Maybe, if I haven't burned them by then.

Finally, I break free, and my mother calls after me, "Don't forget to go around and thank everyone for coming."

I groan, thinking that will take all night, but she's right; I would feel guilty if I didn't talk to everyone I've invited. So by the time I make the rounds with my fake smile, "Thank you for coming!" has been forever tattooed into my psyche. I've managed to snatch only one bacon-wrapped scallop all night, but as I'm heading over to the buffet line, someone taps me on the shoulder.

"Thank you for—" I begin like I'm on crack, desperately salivating for a chicken finger. But at that moment I'm staring right into Pip's blue eyes. I look away and mumble "—coming."

He's standing with hands in pockets, eyebrows raised, looking very relaxed, considering what's coming tonight. The room is warm, but I find myself shivering. He says, "How are you?"

"Fine," I say. "Did you talk to Cam?"

"Everything is still on plan."

My posture stiffens. "Listen, about that . . . I may have been wrong. I think Cam is meant to be in Otherworld."

He shakes his head. "No. I spoke to Cam. He wants to be with you."

I didn't realize Pip could be that persuasive. "Then we need to talk to him, to tell him—"

He puts his hand out for me to stop. "There is nothing to tell him. He is positive he wants to stay with you."

"No, you don't get it. It won't work. My visions are always right. The one I had of you walking in leaves—it's right. So the plan will fail. We should just give up now, before Dawn does something that—"

He shakes his head. "You're letting your visions guide you again?"

"No, you don't understand. I want. . . ," I begin. How can I tell him? Here he is, ever so willing to go back to Otherworld, his own personal hell. He never fought it, despite what Dawn said about him being infatuated with me. Is it just because I asked? He's so willing to do whatever I say, just because I ask it of him? So why doesn't he fight? If he cares about me, why is he so willing to leave? My throat closes.

We stand there awkwardly for a moment, and finally he leans in and says, "I was wondering if you would dance with me."

It's only then I notice we're on the dance floor. "You know my track record with that," I mumble, even though something in me wants desperately to feel the warmth of his arms around my body.

"No tango, then. You can choose."

It feels very fairy tale to me, like everyone in the room has disappeared and it's only him, extending his hand out to me. I guess if this were a fairy tale, I'd know more dances. But as it is, I shrug and say, "Okay. Hug-and-sway."

He raises his eyebrows. "Hug-and . . . ?"

"Trust me, you'll get it."

I pull him to the center of the floor and place his hands around my waist. Then I put my hands on his shoulders, so that there is still a nice, respectable distance between us. Though Evil Morgan wants to pull him against me, I control her, since she would have gotten me into *so* much trouble by now. "Now we just sway," I instruct.

"I see," he says, as if it takes more than two brain cells to master. "Like this?"

"You're a natural," I say. Now that we're this close, I have trouble looking him in the eye. I inch my gaze up, to stabbing blue eyes that obviously have no problem meeting mine, then decide it's too risky and focus on the next-best thing, his nostril. Nostrils are not at all sexy. But his, perfectly round, without a trace of nose hair, kind of is. . . .

Control. Find your Zen, Morgan.

And yet, still I find myself tightening my grip around his neck, moving nearer. I feel the stubble of his chin against my cheek and his breath in my ear. I don't want it to stop, ever, so I rest my head on his shoulder. It's so comfortable, as if I belong there. How can he not feel this, too?

But that's when I open my eyes and focus on Eden. She's standing just a few yards away, in her own hug-and-sway with John, but they're completely still. Gaping at me. Eden mouths, "What the hell are you—"

I snap my head up and pull away from him. "You're leaving tonight," I squeak out, my lower lip trembling.

He nods, confusion dawning on his face, and tries to pull me toward him. "I know. We're just dancing."

Is that all we're doing? Why does it feel like so much more to me? And why doesn't it to him?

"Why do you want to leave me?"

It's only then I notice a fresh outbreak of tears on my cheeks. Pip puts his palms out in front of him to stop me. "Okay. Shh. Calm down."

A tingle runs down my neck. I push on his chest and say, "I've got to go," then hurry out to the lobby, my lungs burning for air. It's only 11:15, but when I run out to the balcony, I gasp like a baby taking its first breath.

The rain has let up, and the moon is peeking through a small, square cutout of clouds. Out in this silver light, it's finally peaceful. The balcony is encased in gleaming white marble, and climbing along every inch of the walls is ivy. There are giant stone fountains filled with white chrysanthemums, and I think that if I hide behind one of them, I might never have to go back inside.

"I'm sorry. Did I do something wrong?"

Pip is standing next to me. I've been so busy trying to catch my breath, I'm not sure how he got here. "Go away. Just . . ."

I expect him to turn and leave, tail between his legs, as always. But instead, he stands firm. "No."

I look up at him. "What?"

He's not listening. He's staring at the ground, the dumb guy, totally ignoring me. Before I can grab him by the shoulders, turn him away, and shout, "March!" he says softly, "Those thoughts you were having. The ones you talked about last night. Were they about me?"

I freeze, then hug my shoulders. "No, I—"

"Because I've had some about you."

I'm still trying to come up with something, other than him, that those thoughts could have been about, so I don't quite hear him. "Really?"

"Actually, more than some. Every night, even since before I left Otherworld. Every night," he says, shaking his head. He puts his finger to his temple and says, "It's like you've been in here forever."

My heart begins to beat wildly as I realize that, yes, that's exactly how it feels. It feels like I've known him just as long as, if not longer than, I've known Cam. How is that possible?

"Then why are you so willing to leave me?" I ask.

He sits beside me, a grim smile on his face, and touches my arm. "You think I want to leave?"

"You never fought against it. You just accepted it so easily. Too easily."

The moon disappears, and a thin drizzle starts, casting an eerie fog over the balcony. I turn toward him, and his eyes are molten, intense. I can barely recognize that look. Things have always been a controlled blaze for Cam and me; the fire has never burned beyond that. Not like this. Not so that I feel every hair on my body standing on end, not so that I forget where I am, who I am. "But . . . isn't this wrong?" are all the words my mouth can form.

He isn't listening, because he puts a hand under my chin and tilts it to him, and when our lips touch, there's a heat I haven't felt before, ever. He tastes like mint and his lips are as soft as Cam's, but this kiss is different, more unsure. I touch his cheek, softly, and he pulls away. That's when I spot, out of the corner of my eye, a cloud of deep blackness on the verge of covering us. Pip must see it too, because he grabs my wrist and pulls me out of the way before a giant tree branch can slam down onto the balcony, shattering with a deafening crack.

"Dawn," he shouts, ushering me to a corner of the balcony. "She did that."

I stand there, dazed, as a torrent of hail begins to fall. At first, it's only small bits, but soon, there are tennis balls. He pulls me under an eave and hovers before me like a shield. Protecting me.

"This is bad" are the only words I can get out. "We have to make her stop."

He wipes his mouth with his hand and looks down at me. "I am sorry. I don't know what I was thinking. Tell me what you want me to do, and I will do it."

"For true love, right?" I mutter as the shards of ice crash around us. "There you go, sacrificing yourself again."

He looks confused.

"Why does it have to be up to me? Why don't you tell me what *you* want, for once?"

{239}

He cowers like a wounded animal. "Are you angry at me?"

I'm only then aware that I've been raising my voice. "Yes, I am. If you want me, why don't you say you do? Why do you just sit there and let yourself be taken advantage of?"

"Because I want you to be happy," he murmurs, looking stricken. "Cam makes you happy. You love him, and—"

"I love you, you idiot," I shout at him, poking him so fiercely that he collapses, limp, on a stone bench. And it's only when I say it aloud that I know, for sure, that it's true. "I love you. I love you. Do you hear me?"

As suddenly as it began, the storm stops, and an eerie silence prevails. Pip is staring up at me, expressionless, when I hear a noise coming from the ivy-draped back entrance, and we both turn.

Standing there among the shadows, looking small and vulnerable, is Cam.

48

CAM WALKS TOWARD us, hands almost elbow-deep in his pockets. For once in our lives, his expression is completely unreadable to me.

I open my mouth to speak, but before I can, Pip begins to moan, a low, gurgling sound filling his throat. We both turn in time to see a tendril of ivy snake around his neck, pulling itself tighter, so that his face begins to redden. Immediately, I rush to his side and begin to claw at it.

"Dawn!" Cam shouts to the pink cloud swirling in the air above us. "Stop it!"

It's tightly around his neck, digging into his skin. Pip is clawing, too, but it's useless. As soon as I think it's about to loosen, another strand slinks forward and wraps around his leg, dragging him toward the side of the building. I grasp his hand to keep him with me, but he's being pulled, his feet etching two trails in the hail-covered marble floor. "Cam!" I yell at him. "She's got to stop."

I look at Pip, whose face is losing all expression. He's still gagging, but his eyes are closed. There isn't much time. "Please, don't," I whisper helplessly.

Dawn appears from behind the fountain, navigating between hailstones with her four-inch heels. "Cameron," she says, almost pleadingly, "don't hate me."

"Let him go!" Cam and I shout at her in unison.

Cam rushes her, fists clenched, growling, "You promised!" but she simply extends one manicured finger at him, and he freezes in place.

"I promised I wouldn't try to harm Morgan," she says to him. "I never said anything about the slave boy. I'm sorry, Cameron, that it has come to this. I really wished you wouldn't fight it."

I find myself sprawled out on the marble, Pip's lifeless body by my side. "Please don't hurt him," I beg. "I'll do whatever you say."

Dawn sighs. She looks up at the moon and says, "It's Cameron who has to agree."

I look at Cam, whose face is still frozen in a scowl. I see a softness in his eyes, and bit by bit, life returns to his face and limbs again. He searches my face, and I nod at him, willing him to answer her, bring this nightmare to an end. Then he turns to Dawn and says, "I agree to come with you."

I exhale, both in fear and relief. Somehow, I'd never thought I'd hear those words.

But now I know it's meant to be.

"Perfect," she says. The ivy noose loosens around Pip's neck.

His face is cold and white, like the moon. As I touch it, she continues. "I knew Morgan would sacrifice anything to come to that slave's rescue. I think that of all the many weaknesses humans have, love is the greatest."

I can hear Cameron breaking free from the spell behind me. He huddles over my shoulder. "Is he okay?"

"I don't know. I think he needs an ambulance."

Dawn puts a hand on Cam's shoulder and says, "My king, are you ready?"

"One sec," he says. He makes a move to wave her away, and that's when we both notice it. There's a bright purple flame on the tip of each of his fingers.

"What is that?" I murmur, unable to break my stare.

He reaches into the pocket of his jacket and pulls out the wristwatch I'd given him earlier today. He shows it to me. "Midnight."

"Your powers?"

He shrugs. "Let's see." He reaches down and touches Pip on the hand. Immediately, Pip's body starts to glisten in yellow light from head to toe, and he begins to stir. As Pip's eyelids flutter, Cam, the great king of Otherworld, proclaims, "Whoa."

"'Whoa' is right," I say. I stare at Cam, breathless, as the light envelops him, stretching around his body. As a fairy, he's more beautiful than he ever was in human form.

"I guess I need to go," he says.

"The portal is open?" I ask. "Where?"

"It's not a physical one, Boo. You can't see it." We both turn to look at Pip, whose face is beginning to recapture a bit of the color it had lost. He says, "It's okay, you know."

"What do you mean?"

He takes me to the bench and sits down beside me. The moon has made a reappearance, and he tilts his head up to it. "You and Pip."

I catch a sob in my throat. "You're not angry?"

He shakes his head. "This was supposed to happen. Pip was always supposed to have been in my place. Now, everything is right."

I sigh. "No, if everything were right, I'd still have you. I want you here, with me."

He puts his hands around mine, and they feel fragile and small, like dolls' hands. "But I *am* a fairy. Part of me has always wanted to be in Otherworld. I've even dreamed about it."

"You never told me that."

He says, "It's my home."

"And this isn't?"

"No, not anymore. The only thing that would keep me here is you. I'd never leave if you didn't want me to. But I never doubted that you would be fine."

"I don't know about . . . ," I begin, but my voice trails off when I realize he's right.

"The point is, stop doubting yourself. You can do anything you want to do. And you don't need me for that. You never did."

I feel a tear slide down my cheek. "You know I love you. One, two, three," I say, bringing the middle three fingers to my lips.

He grins, takes my hand, and kisses it. "And four, five, six. And seven, eight, nine. And on and on. I know. And I do, too. No matter what world I'm in."

We lean our heads together, and our kiss is shaky and wet, because I'm crying so hard that my whole body heaves with every breath.

"I have to go now," he says.

"They say I won't remember you tomorrow." I hold tight to his shirt. "But I will. I know I will."

He stands up. "I left you a birthday present back home."

And with that, he lets go of my hands. I can still feel them smooth in my own when he fades slowly away, and then the drizzle swirls, ghostlike, through the air that enveloped him.

49

THE MORNING SUN filters through the blinds when I wake that Saturday. I'm wearing my pajamas and my face has been scrubbed clean, but everything about the night before is a haze. The party seems like it happened decades ago. I can't recall returning to the party, the music dwindling into the night, saying goodbye to any of the guests. All I can remember are disjointed flashes of the car ride home, the side of my head pressed against the cool window, someone's arms around me. Feeling drowsy but comfortable. Lucky. Safe.

I pull up on my elbows and immediately see it, a little box almost hidden by a big pink bow on my nightstand, right next to the roller coaster picture. I untie the bow and open the lid, and find a beautiful, solid-gold fortune cookie on a chain. Lifting it from its cotton gauze bed and turning it in my fingers, I see a hinge in the center. I slowly open the cookie and pull out a message that says, MORGAN SPARKS CAN DO ANYTHING.

I smile for a moment, then lean back in my bed, savoring it. Yes, at this moment, I feel like I can do anything. And maybe it's because I can't remember the responsibilities of yesterday, but it feels like so much more. I'm sixteen. The world is bright and filled with possibilities.

I see more markings on the back of the paper, so I turn it over and read: MAGIC NUMBERS: 1-2-3.

I look at it. Look away. Then look back again. For some reason, it feels like there is a deeper meaning there.

Throwing on my hoodie and jeans, I fasten the chain around my neck and head to the stairs. When I'm halfway down, I grin. Standing there, looking out the window, wearing a baseball cap and jeans and looking utterly scrumptious, is Pip. I feel like I haven't seen him in ages, so I shout, "Hey, you," from the top step as I bound down to meet him.

He turns, and automatically I jump into his arms and give him a long, lingering kiss. His arms around me, that woodsy-clean scent I've come to know and love—it all feels so comfortable, so perfect. "You know, I've wanted to do that forever."

"Morgan"—he laughs—"I saw you last night."

"I know," I say, pulling him to me.

"Are you ready to go?" he murmurs, snuggling into my hair.

I pull the necklace from against my neck and hold it up to him. "Look."

He gives me a questioning glance. "A fortune cookie? Who gave you that?"

In a glimmer, I remember the name. It comes flooding back,

everything, so much so that my heart jumps. Breathlessly, I say, "Cam."

Pip's face is blank. "Who?"

"Cam." I repeat the name again and again. "He's in Otherworld. Don't you remember?"

He squints at me, confused but still grinning. "You've been reading too many fantasy books, I think."

But I know it wasn't fantasy. I know it was real. And I remember.

Not so much the past, but the way I felt when we were together.

It was a feeling like I could do anything.

It's still here.

And I know that's because Cam is looking out for me.

CYN BALOG is a normal, everyday Jersey girl who believes magical things can happen to us when we least expect them. She lives in Pennsylvania with her husband and young daughter. Both are one hundred percent human, or so she thinks. *Fairy Tale* is her first novel.